D1334939

THE COLOURS OF SPACE

'Bart listen to me,' the stranger whispered, in a harsh fast voice. 'Go along with this, or we're both dead!'

When Bart Steele goes to the Earth spaceport to meet his father for the first time in five years, he doesn't realise that his life will never be the same again. Half-Mentorian by birth, he is able to understand and co-exist with the Lhari, the non-human species which has a stranglehold on space travel.

Bart overhears the Lhari at the spaceport discussing the need to intercept an incoming passenger on his father's flight and is stunned to discover that this is a friend of his father. Before he has time to take stock, Bart finds himself a fugitive on an outgoing flight to Capella and his father's friend dead on the runway...

THE COLOURS OF SPACE

AN EPIC OF SPACE ADVENTURE
from the bestselling author of
WEB OF DARKNESS:

'Marion Zimmer Bradley has always
chosen to write action-adventure stories
of pure entertainment and can be relied
upon for good backgrounds, characters,
cultures that are colourful, and well
resolved plots. Her work is recommended
to all readers.'

Lester del Rey

'Action SF with a good deal of swash-
buckling.'

The SF Encyclopedia

Marion Zimmer Bradley lives in Cali-
fornia, with her husband and two
children. She is the celebrated author of
a number of Science Fiction titles. WEB
OF DARKNESS is published by New
English Library.

DEDICATION to David Stephen

First published in the USA 1983 by the
Donning Company/Publishers

First published in Great Britain in 1989
by Lightning

British Library C.I.P.

Bradley, Marion Zimmer, *1930–*
  [The colors of space].
  The colours of space.
  I. [The colors of space]
  II. Title 813'.54[F]

ISBN 0 340 49685 1

Printed and bound in Great Britain
for Hodder and Stoughton
Paperbacks, a division of Hodder and
Stoughton Ltd., Mill Road,
Dunton Green, Sevenoaks, Kent
TN13 2YA. (Editorial Office:
47 Bedford Square, London
WC1B 3DP) by Cox & Wyman Ltd.,
Reading.

THE COLOURS
OF SPACE

Marion Zimmer Bradley

Hodder and Stoughton

Chapter One

The Lhari spaceport didn't belong on Earth.

Bart Steele had thought that, a long time ago, when he first saw it. He had been just twelve years old then, and all excited about seeing Earth for the first time – Earth, the legendary home of mankind before the Age of Space, the planet of Bart's far-back ancestors. And the first thing he'd seen on Earth, when he got off the starship, was the Lhari spaceport.

And he'd thought, right then; *it doesn't belong on Earth*.

He'd said so to his father, and his father's face had gone strange, bitter and remote.

'A lot of people would agree with you, son,' Captain Rupert Steele had said softly. 'The trouble is, if the Lhari spaceport wasn't on Earth – we wouldn't be on Earth either. Remember that.'

Bart remembered it, five years later, as he got off the strip of moving sidewalk; he turned to wait for Tom Kendron, who was getting his baggage off the centre strip of the moving roadway. Bart Steele and Tom Kendron had graduated together, the day before, from the Space Academy on Earth. Now Tom, who had been born on the ninth planet of the star Capella, was taking the Lhari starship to his faraway home; and Bart's father was coming in to Earth, by the same ship, to meet his son.

Five years, Bart thought. *I wonder if Dad will know me?*

5

'Let me give you a hand with that stuff, Tom.'

'I can manage,' Tom chuckled, hefting the plastic case. 'They don't allow you much baggage weight on the Lhari ships – certainly not more than I can handle.'

The two young men stood in front of the spaceport gate for a minute. Over the gate, which was high and pointed and made of some clear colourless material like glass, was a jagged symbol like a flash of lightning. Bart knew, as everyone knew, that this was the sign, in the Lhari language, for the home world of the Lhari.

They walked through the pointed glass gate and stood for a moment, by mutual consent, looking down over the vast expanse of the Lhari spaceport.

This had once been a great desert. Now it was all floored in with a strange substance that was neither glass, metal nor concrete. It looked like gleaming crystal, and in the glaring light of the noon sun overhead, it gave back the glare in a million rainbow flashes. Tom blinked, put his hands up to his eyes to shade them, and said through his spread fingers, 'The Lhari must have funny eyes, if they can stand all this glare!'

Inside the glass gate was a barricade, and a uniformed guard handed them each a pair of dark glasses. He said, as he had far too often in the last half hour or so, 'Put them on now, boys. And don't look directly at the ship when it lands, even with your glasses on.'

Tom hooked the earpieces of the dark glasses over his ears, and sighed with relief. Bart frowned at the glasses, but finally put them on. Bart could stand a lot of light; he had been born on the third planet of Vega, a star many times brighter than the sun of Earth. And Bart's mother had been a Mentorian – from the planet, Mentor, of the star Deneb, a thousand times brighter than the sun. Bart had her eyes. But Mentorians weren't popular on Earth, and Bart had learned to be quiet

about his mother. He put on the dark glasses and the glare subsided to a pale gleam.

Far out in the very centre of the spaceport, a high, clear-glass skyscraper rose, catching the sunlight in a million colours. All around the building, small copters and robocabs veered, discharging passengers, and the moving sidewalks were crowded with people coming and going. Here and there in the crowd, the exceedingly tall figures of the Lhari stood out in their brilliant metallic cloaks.

'Well, how about going down?' Tom glanced impatiently at his timepiece. 'Less than half an hour before the starship touches down.'

'All right. We can get a sidewalk over here.' Reluctantly, Bart tore his eyes away from the fascinating spectacle, and followed Tom to one of the moving sidewalks. It bore them down a long, sloping ramp towards the floor of the spaceport, and sped towards the glass skyscraper; came to rest at the wide pointed doors, depositing them in the middle of the crowd. The jagged lightning-flash was there, over the doors of the building, and the words:

THIS, BY THE GRACE OF THE LHARI, IS THE DOORWAY TO ALL THE STARS.

Bart remembered, as if it were yesterday, how he and his father had first passed through this doorway. And his father, looking up, had said under his breath, 'Not for always, son. Believe me, not for always. Some day there will be a *real* doorway to the stars – and the Lhari won't be standing in the door, holding it open just a crack, the way they do now.'

Inside the building, it was searingly bright. The high open rotunda was full of mirrors and glass ramps running up and down, moving staircases, confusing signs, and flashing lights that didn't mean a thing to

7

Bart. The place was crowded with men from all over the planet, all wearing dark glasses except for the Lhari.

Tom said, 'I have to have my ticket stamped.'

Bart nodded. 'Meet you on the upper level,' and got on a moving staircase that soared slowly upwards, past level after level, each one crowded with new things, to the information desk on the topmost mezzanine.

The staircase moved slowly, and Bart had plenty of time to see everything.

On the step immediately in front of Bart, two Lhari were standing. With their backs turned to him, they might almost have been men, unusually tall, unusually thin, but men. Then he mentally amended that. The Lhari had two arms, two legs and a head apiece – they looked that much like men. Their faces had two eyes, two ears, a nose and a mouth. But it ended there.

They had curious pale silvery grey skin and pure white hair rising in what looked like a feathery crest. Their eyes, beneath gracefully sloped eyebrows, were long and slanting; their foreheads were high and narrow, the nose delicately thin and chiselled, with curious vertically-slit nostrils; the ears long, pointed and lobeless. The mouth looked almost human, and the teeth, but the chins were far too pointed to be human. The hands would almost pass inspection as human hands – except for the long, triangular nails, curved over the fingertips like the claws of a cat. They wore skin-tight clothes of silky metallic cloth, and long gleaming silver capes. They looked very strange and unearthly, and in their own way they were beautiful.

The two Lhari in front of Bart had been talking softly in their shrill twittering speech which Bart had an odd talent for imitating; but now, as the hum of the crowds on the upper levels grew louder, they raised their voices somewhat, and Bart could hear what they were saying. He was a little surprised to find that he could still

8

understand the Lhari language. He hadn't heard a word of it in years – not since his Mentorian mother died. He didn't feel any guilt about eavesdropping. The Lhari would never guess that he could understand their speech. Not one human in a million could speak or understand more than a dozen words of Lhari – except Mentorians.

'Do you really think that *human* –' the first Lhari spoke the word as if it were a filthy insult, 'will have the daring to come in by this ship?'

'No reasonable being can tell what *humans* will do,' said the second Lhari, whose lined, deeply wrinkled face proclaimed him the elder, 'and very few can tell what the Port Authorities will do. If the message had only reached us sooner, it would have been easier – now I suppose it will have to clear through a dozen officials. Remember that we have only a description – he might be anyone, and we can't risk alarming *all* the passengers, not yet at least. We don't want to trouble innocent people. But if he does, believe me, our port authorities will deal with him!'

'I can't understand how such a thing ever happened,' twittered the first Lhari in agitation, 'or how he ever managed to get away. The whole crew of that ship should be sent to pick fungus for forty cycles!'

'Oh, they have been punished, Margil!' The old Lhari made the soft whistling sound that served the Lhari for laughter. 'Believe me, they won't let *that* happen again on any Lhari ship.'

'But if this thing became known, even to the Mentorians, it would be a catastrophe,' the first Lhari said. 'What worries me is the possibility that he may have communicated with others before he boarded this ship – if he did. The bungling fools who let him get away, can't even be sure –'

'Do not speak of it here!' said the second Lhari

sharply. 'There are Mentorians in the crowd who might understand us!' He turned suddenly and looked straight at Bart, and Bart felt as if the slanted strange grey eyes were looking right through to his bones. The Lhari said, in Universal, 'Who are you, boy? What iss your business here?'

'My father's coming in on this ship,' Bart said politely, 'I'm looking for the information desk.'

'Up there,' said the old Lhari, pointing with his clawed fingers, and lost interest in Bart. He said to his companion, in their own language, 'Always, I regret these episodes. I have no malice against humans. I suppose even this Vegan that we are seeking has young, and a mate, who will regret his loss.'

'Then he should not have pried into Lhari matters,' said the young Lhari fiercely. As the soaring staircase swooped up to the top level, they stepped off, and mingled swiftly with the crowd, being lost to sight.

Bart whistled in dismay as he got off and went towards the information desk. A Vegan! Some poor guy from his own planet was in trouble with the Lhari, right enough! He felt a cold, crawling chill down in his insides. The Lhari had spoken regretfully, but as he'd speak of a fly he wanted to swat. Sooner or later you got down to it: they just weren't *human!*

Here on Earth, nothing much could happen of course. They wouldn't let the Lhari hurt anyone – then Bart remembered his Academy course in Universal Law. The Lhari spaceport on every planet, by treaty, was Lhari territory. When you shipped out on a Lhari ship, you were automatically subject to the laws of the Lhari Empire.

Tom stepped off another moving sidewalk and rejoined him. He said, 'The ship's on time – they told me, down there, that it reported in at Luna City a few minutes ago. Shall we get something to drink?'

There was a refreshment stand on this level. They debated briefly between orange juice and a drink with a Lhari name that meant, simply, *cold sweet*, and finally decided to try it. The name, Bart decided as he sipped it, was descriptive; it was very cold, very sweet, and indescribably delicious.

Tom asked, 'Does this come from the Lhari worlds, I wonder?'

'I suppose it's some kind of synthetic,' Bart said.

Tom hesitated, staring at his glass. 'I suppose it won't *hurt* us?'

Bart laughed. 'They wouldn't serve it to us here, if it would! No, men and Lhari are alike in a lot of ways. They eat the same food, for instance. Breathe the same air.' Their bodies were adjusted to about the same gravity. The Lhari were warm-blooded – in fact, you couldn't tell Lhari blood from human, except under a microscope. Doctors had found out, in the terrible Orion Spaceport Wreck sixty years ago, that blood plasma from humans could be used for wounded Lhari, and vice versa, though it wasn't safe to transfuse whole blood.

And yet, for all their likeness to humans, the Lhari were *different*.

Bart sipped his drink, seeing himself in the mirror behind the refreshment stand; a tall teenager, looking older than his seventeen years. He was lithe and well-muscled from five years of sports and acrobatics at the Space Academy; he had curling red hair and grey eyes, and he was almost as tall as a Lhari. He wondered again, with a little flick of excitement, *will Dad know me? I was just a kid when he left me here five years ago, and now I'm grown up*.

Tom turned around and grinned at him. 'What are you going to do, now that we're through with our so-called education?'

'What do you think? Go back to Vega with Dad, on the Lhari ships – and help him run Vega Interplanetary,' Bart told him. 'Why else would I bother with all that astrogation and mathematics?'

'You're the lucky one,' Tom said enviously, 'with your father owning a dozen ships! He must be almost as rich as the Lhari!'

Bart shook his head. 'It's not that easy,' he said. 'Space travel between planets is small stuff, these days. All the real trading and travel goes to the Lhari ships.'

It was a sore point with everyone. Thousands of years ago, men had spread out from Earth – first to the planets, then to the nearer stars – crawling in ships that could travel no faster than the speed of light. They had believed it was an absolute limit – that nothing in the universe could exceed the speed of light. It took years to go from Earth to the nearest star.

But they'd done it. From the nearer stars, they had sent out colonizing ships all through the galaxy. A few of them vanished, and were never heard of again. But some of them made it, and in a few centuries man had spread over hundreds of stars.

And then mankind first met the people of the Lhari.

It was a big universe, with measureless millions of stars. It wasn't surprising that the Lhari, who had only been travelling space for a few thousand years themselves, had never come across humans before. But they were delighted to meet another intelligent race – and it was awfully profitable.

Because men were still held, mostly, to the planets in their own star systems. Ships travelling between the stars, by L-drive, were rare – and ruinously expensive. But the Lhari had had the warpdrive, and, almost overnight, everything was changed. By warpdrive, hundreds of times faster than light, the years-long trip between Vega and Earth was reduced to about three

12

weeks, at a price anyone could pay. Mankind could travel and trade all over the universe – but they did it by the grace of the Lhari, on Lhari ships. The Lhari had an absolute, unbreakable monopoly on star travel. Bart grinned bitterly at Tom and said, 'The Lhari get all the business, of course. They're the richest, most arrogant race in the Universe!'

'That's what hurts,' Tom said. 'It wouldn't do us any good, even if we had the warpdrive. Humans can't stand it, unless they're in suspended animation.'

Bart nodded, remembering. The Lhari ships travelled at normal speeds, like the planetary ships, inside each star-system. Then, at the borders of the vast gulf of emptiness between stars, they went into warpdrive – but first, every human aboard the ship was given the coldsleep treatment that placed them in suspended animation and permitted their bodies to endure the warpdrive.

Bart finished his drink and turned to look out over the crowds. There was an increasing bustle below them, a frantic hurry in the crowded people below, that told him time must be getting short. A tall, impressive-looking Lhari strode through the crowd, gleaming in metallic gold cloak and tights, followed at a respectful distance by two Mentorians; tall, redheaded humans, wearing metallic cloaks like those of the Lhari. Tom nudged Bart, and his face was bitter.

'Look at those lousy Mentorians! How can they do it? They're as human as we are – and yet they're like traitors! Crawling to the Lhari, that way! *Slaves* of the Lhari!'

'It's not that way at all,' Bart said slowly. 'I know; my mother was a Mentorian, remember. She took five cruises with the Lhari, before she married my father. And she didn't think the Lhari were so bad. They've given us space travel.'

Tom looked abashed; then he sighed. 'I guess I'm jealous,' he admitted. 'When I think that the Mentorians can sign on the Lhari ships as crew – and you and I will never pilot a ship between the stars! Your *mother* shipped with the Lhari? What did she do?'

'She was a mathematician,' Bart said slowly. 'The Lhari use human maths – you learned in school, of course, that before they met up with man, the Lhari used a navigational system as clumsy as Roman numerals. You have to admire them for that. And, of course, you know that the Lhari have different eyesight than we do. Among other things, they're colour blind.'

'Colour blind!'

'That's right,' Bart said. 'Their eyes can't tell the colours apart, just shades of black or white or grey. You know humans, before space, used to use some animals who were more sensitive to impure air – and when they keeled over, time for humans to get out! So the Lhari found out that it was useful to have some humans on their crew, just to distinguish different parts of the spectrum. And, of course, they use Mentorians for interpreters and translators when dealing with humans.'

Tom followed the Mentorians, enviously and resentfully, with his eyes. 'The fact is, I'd ship out with the Lhari myself if I could. Just to travel between the stars. Would you?'

Bart's mouth twisted in a smile. 'I could,' he said. 'I'm half Mentorian.'

'Why don't you? I would!'

'Oh, no you wouldn't,' Bart said softly. 'Not even very many of the Mentorians will. You see, the Lhari don't trust humans too much – not even Mentorians. And in the early days, men were always planting spies on the Lhari ships, to try and steal the secret of the warpdrive. They never managed. But now Lhari give the Mentorians what amounts to a brainwashing, before

14

they sign on – and before they sign off. They can't reveal anything that's important. My mother was one, I told you. Oh, she could tell me little things. For instance, in trading jewels, the Lhari can't tell a diamond from a ruby except by spectrographic analysis. That sort of thing. Only she got tired of losing her memories every year or so.'

Tom shuddered, but before he could answer, a series of warning bells and buzzers exploded all over the building.

'The ship must be coming in,' Bart said.

'I guess I'd better go and get ready to check in,' Tom said. He stuck out his hand. 'Well – Bart, I guess this is where we say goodbye.'

They shook hands, their eyes meeting for a moment in honest grief through their mutual excitement at the new life they were entering. They both knew that their parting was, in some indefinable way, the end of boyhood.

'Good luck, Tom. I – hope we see each other again.'

'Me, too. I'm going to miss you. You'll have to come out to the Capella system, some time,' Tom said. 'So long, Bart.'

They wrung each other's hands again, hard. Then Tom picked up his luggage, and disappeared down a sloping ramp towards an enclosure marked PASSENGERS ONLY.

Warning bells rang again. The glare intensified, until even Bart closed his eyes, but he opened them again, unable to resist. Outside the glass walls he saw the glow in the sky. It was unbearable but he looked anyhow, making out the strange shape of the Lhari ship from the stars.

It was huge and strange, the shape curiously indistinct, glowing with colours Bart had never seen before and would never see anywhere else. It settled down slowly, softly, and sat there enormous, silent, vibrating, glowing; then, swiftly, faded to white-hot, glowing blue, dulling down through the visible spectrum to red. At last it was just gleaming glassy Lhari-metal colour again. High up in the ship's side a yawning gap slid open, extruding long stairsteps, and men and Lhari began to descend.

Bart ran down the ramp and surged out on the field with the crowd. His eyes, alert for his father's tall figure, noted with surprise that the steps down from the starship were guarded by four cloaked Lhari, each with a Mentorian interpreter. They were stopping each person who got off the starship, asking for his identity cards or papers. He recognized the old Lhari he had seen on the escalator, and realised that he was seeing a segment of the same confusing drama. He wished he knew what it was all about.

He had no idea how soon his wish was to be granted.

All over the spaceport, passengers were greeting little groups who had come to meet them. Bart saw a man in the dress of a Centaurian rush to meet a tall girl and grab her in a hard hug, and thought, *she's met her father. But where's mine?*

The crowd was thinning now. Robocabs were swerving in, hovering to pick up people from the crowd, veering away. The gap in the starship's side was closing, and still Bart had not seen, anywhere, the tall, slender form of Captain Steele. Was there another port on the far side of the ship? Bart walked worriedly through the edge of the crowd.

One of the Lhari checking papers stopped, fixed him with an inscrutable grey stare, but finally turned away again. Bart began to really worry. Captain Steele would never miss his ship! But he saw only one disembarking passenger who had not already been surrounded by a welcoming crowd of relatives. He was wearing Vegan clothes, but he wasn't Bart's father. He was a fat little man, with ruddy cheeks, and a fringe of curling grey hair all around his bald dome. Bart looked at him, and thought, maybe he'd know if there was another Vegan on the ship. I could ask him –

The Lhari checking papers was watching the little fat man – and Bart realised, suddenly, that the little fat man was staring at *him*, at Bart! He returned the man's smile, rather hesitantly; then blinked, for the fat man was coming straight towards him.

'Hello, son,' he said loudly, to someone who must have been right behind Bart – for he was looking straight in Bart's direction. Then, as two of the Lhari started towards him, the fat man did an incredible thing. He stretched out his two hands and grabbed Bart, hard.

'Well, boy, you've sure grown,' he said, in a loud, cheerful tone. 'But you're not too grown-up to give your old Dad a good hug, are you?' He pulled Bart roughly into his arms. Bart started to twist away and stammer that the strange man had made a mistake, but the fat man gripped painfully on his wrist with unexpected strength.

'Bart, listen to me,' the stranger whispered, in a harsh fast voice, 'Go along with this, or we're both dead! Keep your head! Those two Lhari are watching us, so call me Dad, good and loud, if you want to live! Because, believe me, your life's in danger – right now!'

Chapter Two

For a moment Bart was too surprised to move or speak. Pulled off balance in the fat man's hug, he remained perfectly still, while the man said again in that loud, jovial voice, 'How you've grown!' He let him go, stepping back a pace or two, and whispered urgently, 'Say something! And take that stupid look off your face!'

And as he stepped back, Bart saw his eyes. In the chubby, good-natured red face, the stranger's eyes were half-mad with fear.

In a split second, Bart remembered the two Lhari, talking about some fugitive. He realised that he had been catapulted right into the middle of the story – and in that minute Bart Steele grew up. He acted quickly without thinking about it. He stepped towards the man and took him by the shoulders, seeing over his shoulder the two Lhari – four of them now, two on each side – closing in swiftly from each direction.

'Dad, you sure surprised me,' he said, trying to keep his voice from shaking the way that fat man's shoulders were shaking. 'It's been a long time, I'd half forgotten what – what you looked like. How – how are you coming along? Have a good trip?'

'Just about like always,' the little fat man said. He was trembling and breathing hard, but his voice did not tremble, and it sounded loud and cheerful. 'Solid comfort. Can't compare with the old *Flyer*, though.' The

Flyer was the chief interplanetary ship owned by Bart's father. 'How's everything here?'

Beads of sweat were standing out on the fat man's ruddy forehead, and his grip on Bart's wrist was so hard that it hurt. Bart, grasping for something to say, said fast and at random, 'I came down here with my friend Tom, he's shipping out on this ship. He's going home to the Capella system. We graduated together –' he swallowed, and the fat man whispered, 'Keep on talking.'

'He – wants to be a spaceman, like me, Dad, it's a shame you couldn't get to my graduation –'

The Lhari had them surrounded now, and were closing in. The fat man swallowed hard a time or two, took a deep breath, and turned around. He said, 'You want something?'

The tallest of the Lhari – the old one, the one with the laugh, the one Bart had heard on the escalator – looked long and hard at Bart. When the Lhari spoke Universal, it sounded sibilant but not nearly so inhuman.

'Could we trrrouble you to ssshow us your papersssss?'

'Sure,' the man said nonchalantly, digging them out and handing them over. Bart saw his father's name printed across the top. The Lhari officer gestured to a Mentorian interpreter.

'What colourrr iss thiss man's hairrr?'

The Mentorian said in Lhari, 'His hair is grey.' He used the Universal word; there were no words for colours in the Lhari language.

'The man we seek has hair of *red*,' said the Lhari. Again the word *red* was in Unversal. 'And he is tall, not fat.'

'The boy is tall and with red hair,' the Mentorian volunteered, and the Lhari made a gesture of disdain. 'This boy is twenty years younger than the man whose description we have. Why did they not give us a picture or at least a name?' He turned to the other Lhari and

19

said in their own shrill speech, 'I suspected this man because he was alone. And this boy had come to meet a father and no father had yet greeted him, so perhaps the father he came to seek was the man we wanted. If so, and we watched the boy, sooner or later the father would seek him out. Ask him –' he gestured, and the Mentorian said, 'Who is this man, you?'

Bart gulped, noticing for the first time the energon-ray beams at the Lhari's belt. He'd heard all about those things. They could kill, or stun. He said, 'This is my father. You want my identity card? My name's Bart Steele.'

The Lhari, with a gesture of disgust, handed back the papers. 'Go, then, father and son,' he said, not unkindly, and turned on his heel. One said, 'Perhaps he is hiding within the ship,' and they converged purposefully on the ladder.

'Let's get going, son,' said the fat, bald little man. His hand shook on Bart's, and Bart thought, if we're lucky we can get out of the port before he faints dead away.

He said, 'I'll get a copter – Dad,' and then, feeling sorry for the strange man, gave him his arm to lean on. He didn't know whether he was worried – or scared. *Where was his father?* Was his father hiding in the ship, and in danger from the Lhari? He wanted to run, to burst away from this man with his father's forged papers, and yet the guy was shaking so hard he couldn't just leave him there. If the Lhari got hold of him, he was a dead man.

A copter swooped down and the man said hoarsely, 'No. A robocab.'

Bart waved the copter away, getting a dirty look from the driver, and punched a button for one of the unmanned robocabs. Inside, the fat man collapsed on the seat, leaning back, puffing. His hand pressed hard to his chest.

'Punch a combo for Denver,' he said hoarsely.

Bart obeyed, automatically. Then he turned on the man.

'It's your game, mister! Now tell me what's going on!' His anxiety spilled over; *'Where is my father?'*

The man did not answer. His eyes were half shut. 'Don't ask me any questions for a minute,' he said, gasping, and fumbled in a pocket. He thumbed a tablet into his mouth and after a minute his harsh breathing quieted a little; but he still looked half dead.

'We're safe – for the minute. Those Lhari – would have cut us down –'

'You, maybe,' Bart said, 'I haven't done anything. Look, you,' he said in sudden rage. 'You owe me some explanations. I went along with you back there because I wouldn't turn anyone over to the Lhari to be cut down and killed. But for all I know, you're a criminal. Why are you travelling with my father's papers? Did you steal his papers to get away from the Lhari? *Where's my father?'*

'It's your father they were looking for, you young fool,' the man said, gasping hard. 'Couldn't you tell from the description? And we've only confused them for a little while. The port authorities haven't cleared *both* descriptions yet. I'm all right – they knew they were looking for a tall redhead, and I'm short and fat. But if you'd refused to play along, they'd have had you watched –'

'Where is my father?'

'I hope I don't know,' the fat man said. 'If he's still where I left him, he's dead. My name is Briscoe,' he added. 'Your father saved my life years ago, never mind how – the less you know, the safer you'll be. He was in disguise, but I recognized him. Well, he gave them the slip, but he was worried about you – afraid, if he didn't turn up on Earth you'd take the first ship back to the Vega system. So he gave me his papers and sent me to

21

warn you –'

Bart shook his head. It was all too much to believe. 'It all sounds incredible,' he said. 'How do I know?'

The man fished in his pocket and took out a blank piece of paper. Bart stared, turning it in his hands. 'What in the –'

'Hold it under the sunlight.'

Bart complied and after a minute, very pale pink lines began to appear against the yellowish paper. 'The Lhari can't see colour,' the man said, 'and there isn't enough difference in intensity here for them to see it even as different shades of grey. Invisible ink.'

The writing was so pale that Bart had trouble making it out. *Bart,* it read, *I send money and instructions by my friend. Do as he says. Don't go home, Dad.*

Bart thrust the paper back at him. 'It doesn't sound like Dad,' he said vehemently, 'It's not like his writing, it could be anybody.' His hand hovered over the robocab controls. 'We're going straight to the police. They won't turn you over to the Lhari, but you can explain to them why you have my father's papers.'

'You young fool, you blithering idiot,' said the fat man, leaning back weakly. 'There's no *time* for all that! Ask me questions! I can prove I know your father!'

'What was my mother's maiden name?'

'Oh, God,' Briscoe said, 'I never saw your mother, I knew him before you were born. Until he told me, I didn't know he'd ever married, or that he had a son. I'd never have known you except that you're the living image of him.' He shook his head, helplessly, and his breathing sounded funny.

'Look,' he said, 'I'm a sick man, I'm going to die. I want to do what I came here to do, just because your father saved my life when I was young and healthy, and gave me twenty good years before I got old and fat and sick. Win or lose, it's nothing to me. I won't live to see you burned down by the Lhari, either way.'

'Don't talk that way,' Bart said, a strange creepy feeling coming over him as he looked at the man's red face. There was a very odd look in the stranger's eyes. 'If you're sick, let me take you to a doctor, then.'

Briscoe did not even hear. 'Wait,' he said suddenly. 'Your father did say something. He said – tell Bart I've gone to look for the eighth colour. Bart will know what I mean by that.'

'That's crazy,' Bart said. It didn't mean anything at all ... and then a memory popped into his head.

He'd only been a little fellow – it was while his mother was still alive. She had been searching her few memories of the Lhari cruises she had made, and she had spoken of the element that fuelled the warpdrive engines. She had said, 'It's a very queer colour, a colour you never saw before. Can you think of a colour that isn't red, orange, yellow, green, blue, violet, indigo, or some combination of them? Well, this isn't any of the colours of the spectrum. It's a real eighth colour.'

And abruptly Bart was convinced. Because only his father would have used that phrase. He had said, once, 'Some day we'll know what that eighth colour is – and then we'll have the secret of the Lhari warpdrive!'

'I see it means something to you,' Briscoe said. 'Now will you do what I tell you?'

'What do you want me to do?' Bart asked.

'Within two hours, they're going to be combing the planet for you,' Briscoe said grimly. He stopped, breathed hard again, and said, 'The authorities of Earth might protect you, but you'd never be able to board a Lhari ship again, and that would mean staying here for the rest of your life. You've got to get out *before* they all start comparing notes. Here – his hand went into his pocket. 'Douse this on your hair. It's a spray – a dye.'

'I don't –'

'Give it here, then!' Impatiently the man took it, pressed a button; Bart gasped, feeling a cold wetness on his head. His hand came away stained black.

'Keep still,' Briscoe said irritably. 'It won't make a difference at this end, maybe, but you'll need it at Procyon.' He thrust some papers into Bart's hand. Then he reached out and pushed the buttons on the robocab's controls. It wheeled so rapidly that Bart fell against the fat man's shoulder; turned back, hovered over the spaceport.

'Look,' Bart said, finding his voice through the confusion of things moving too fast. 'Are you crazy? What do you expect me to do? What are you going to do? Why –'

'I haven't time to argue,' Briscoe said. The robocab swooped down, hovered almost motionless. Suddenly, he turned his head and looked straight into Bart's eyes. In his hoarse, sick, wheezing voice, he said, 'Don't worry about me, Bart. It's all over for me, whatever happens. Just remember this; what your father's doing, is worth doing. If you start stalling, arguing, asking questions, demanding explanations, you can foul it all up.' He closed Bart's fingers roughly over the wallet and the papers he had thrust into them. 'Now. When I stop this cab, jump out. Don't stop to say goodbye, or ask any questions, or anything else. Just get out, walk through the two doors of this building, and straight up the ramp of the ship. Don't let anything stop you, whatever happens. Bart!' Briscoe shook his shoulder. 'Promise me that! Whatever happens, *get on that ship!*'

Bart swallowed. He felt as if he'd been shoved into a silly cops-and-robbers game, but Briscoe's urgency had convinced him. He didn't want to stay here for the rest of his life. He said weakly, 'Dad – ?'

'All I know is that you've got to get in touch with a man called Raynor Three,' Briscoe said.

'Is Dad there? Does he –'

'I don't know. I don't know anything about it,' Briscoe said. His mouth twisted again in that painful gasp. 'Promise? Whatever happens, you'll get on that ship?'

Bart shook his head, bewildered, but under Briscoe's intense stare he finally said, 'Okay, I promise. But listen, can't you tell me –'

'I've told you all I can tell you. Go on – mix in the crowd!' Abruptly, the robocab came to a halt; Briscoe jerked the door open, gave Bart a push, and Bart found himself stumbling out the ramp by the spaceport building. He caught his balance, looked round, and realised that the robocab was already climbing the sky again.

Immediately before him, a neon sign spelled out PASSENGERS ONLY. Behind him someone pushed and said with asperity, 'Where did you learn to handle a robocab? Come on, we haven't got all day!'

Bart blinked, automatically moving forward. The Lhari at the gate by the neon sign held out a disinterested claw and Bart held up what Briscoe had shoved into his hand, only now seeing that it was a thick wallet, a set of identity papers, and a strip of pink tickets.

'Procyon Alpha,' said the Lhari disinterestedly. 'Straight through to the ramp.' He gestured, and Bart gulped. At least he knew where he was going now. He went through the narrow shed, out at the other side, and found himself at the very base of a curving ramp which led up and towards the huge Lhari spaceship. Bart hesitated. In another minute it would be too late; he'd be on his way to a strange world and a strange sun, on what might well prove to be the wild-goose chase of all time, with only the unlikely name of 'Raynor Three' as a clue to what he'd do when he got there.

Someone shouted, 'Will you look at that!' someone

else yelled. 'Is that guy crazy?' Bart stopped, looked up. A robocab was swooping down over the spaceport, coming in wide crazy circles, dipping down, suddenly making a dart, like an enraged wasp, at the little nest of Lhari. They ducked and scattered; the robocab swerved away, hovered, swooped back. This time it knocked one of the Lhari off his feet; Bart stood, his mouth open, as if paralysed. *What was Briscoe doing?*

The fallen Lhari lay without moving. The robocab moved in again, as if for the kill.

Then a beam of light arched from one of the drawn energon-tubes. The robocab glowed briefly red – then seemed to sag, sink together; then puddled, a slag-heap of molten metal on the glassy spaceport floor. A little moan of horror came from the crowd, and Bart felt a sudden, horrible, wrenching sickness. It had been like a game, a silly game of cops and robbers, and suddenly it was as serious as melted death lying there on the spaceport floor. *Briscoe!* The fat man's wheezing words came back; *whatever happens. Promise!*

Someone shoved him and said, 'Come on, friend, they won't hold the ship because some maniac finds a fancy new way to commit suicide,' and Bart, his legs numb, walked up the ramp.

Briscoe had died to give him this chance for escape – and now it was up to him to make it worth having.

Chapter Three

At the top of the ramp a Lhari, in the metallic silky tights but without cape, took a brief glance at his papers; the Mentorian interpreter at his side nodded, and said, 'Go on through.'

Bart passed through the airlock into a brilliantly lighted corridor, flaring with mercury-vapour lamps. He was glad he still had his sunglasses. The space was about half filled with a quickly-moving line of passengers. A woman ahead of him said nervously, 'We won't be drugged and put in coldsleep right away, will we?'

Her companion, evidently a veteran of many trips, shook his head scornfully. 'No, the ship doesn't go into warpdrive until we're past Pluto. Inside a solar system they can't travel any faster than planetary ships. It will be almost a week before coldsleep. I told you this was a pleasure trip!'

Pleasure trip! Bart felt his knees wobbling. What would the people at his rooming house think when he failed to return? He'd had them all ready to expect his father. Where was his father? Suddenly he felt like a small boy again, and his throat hurt, a tight pain behind his eyes. He was a little sick at his stomach, and quite simply scared to death.

Briscoe hadn't been afraid to die. Bart had never seen violent death before. In this civilised world, you didn't.

He knew if he thought hard about Briscoe he'd start bawling like a baby, so he swallowed hard a couple of times, set his chin, clenched his teeth, stiffened his backbone, and thought about a trip to Procyon Alpha.

That meant this ship was bound outward on the Aldebaran run. Before arriving at Procyon, they would make three system stops: Proxima Centauri, which was the jumping-off place for all Earth runs (Sol, of course, was an isolated star at the very edge of the civilised universe), Sirius, Pollux, then Procyon – and afterwards, Capella and Aldebaran.

Bart reached a doorway. He went through, the light dwindled and a Mentorian interpreter said, 'You may remove your dark glasses now.'

Bart handed them over. The Mentorian before him, wearing the white smock of a medical officer, said, 'Kindly remove your belt, shoes, and any other accessories before stepping into the decontamination chamber. They will be separately decontaminated and returned to you. Give me your papers, please.'

With a small twinge of fright, Bart surrendered them; he still had his Academy ID card that identified him as Bart Steele, and his other identifications, and if the Mentorian looked at them, he might wonder – he jolly well *would* wonder – why Bart was carrying two sets of papers!

But the Mentorian took all his pocket paraphernalia with a shrug, dumped it all into a plastic sack, and stapled his ticket number on the outside. 'Just step through there.'

Bart, holding up his trousers with both hands, stepped inside the chamber. It was filled with a faint bluish light; Bart felt a strong tingling and a faint electrical smell, and along his forearms there was a faint prickle where the hairs were all standing on end. He knew that the R-rays were killing all the micro-organisms on his body, so that the disease germs or minute bacteria would not be carried from planet to planet.

The bluish light died. He stepped out, the Mentorian gave him back his shoes and belt (the R-rays were harmless, but would have made the metal so hot that it could give him a bad burn), and handed him the sack of his belongings and a paper cup full of greenish fluid. 'Drink this.'

'What is it?'

The Mentorian medical officer said patiently, 'Remember, the R-rays killed *all* the micro-organisms in your body – even the antibodies that protect you against diseases, and the small yeasts and bacteria that live in your intestines and help digest your food. We kill them all off, then we put back the ones that don't hurt anyone. See?'

The green stuff tasted a little brackish, but Bart got it down all right. He didn't much like the idea of drinking a solution of 'germs', but he knew that was silly. There was a big difference between disease germs and helpful bacteria. Another Mentorian official, this one a young woman, gave him a key with a numbered tag, and a little booklet with WELCOME ABOARD printed on the cover. *Just as if it were a pleasure trip and I was just another tourist.*

The tag was numbered 246-B, and Bart raised his eyebrows. He had never travelled D-class, where the passengers were stowed away in stacked bunks and given coldsleep from the minute they boarded to the minute they disembarked – in D-class, passengers were handled like sacked luggage – but *B-class* was far too expensive for Bart's father's quite modest purse. It wasn't the luxury Class-A, reserved for planetary governors and dignitaries, but it was plenty luxurious. Briscoe had certainly sent him travelling in style! The thought made him remember Briscoe again, and the horrible melted puddle of the robocab, and he shuddered.

B Deck was a long corridor with oval doors; Bart found one numbered 246, and, not surprisingly, the key opened it. It was a comfortable little cabin, about six feet by eight, and he would evidently have it to himself. There was a comfortably big bunk, a light which could be turned on and off instead of the permanent glow-walls of the cheaper classes, a private shower and toilet, and a small placard informing him that passengers in B-Class had the freedom of the Observation Dome and the Recreation Lounge throughout the voyage. There was the usual array of buttons, dispensing synthetic foods, beside the door, in case a passenger preferred privacy or didn't want to bother waiting for food to be served in the dining hall.

A buzzer went off, and a Mentorian voice announced, 'Five minutes to Room Check. Passengers will please remove all metal in their clothing and deposit in the lead drawers. Passengers will please recline in their bunks and fasten the retaining straps before the steward arrives. Repeat, passengers -'

Bart took off his belt again, stuck it and his cufflinks in the drawer, and lay down. Then, in a sudden panic, he got up again. His papers as Bart Steele were still in his pants pocket. He got them out, sorted them out from his new papers, and, with a feeling rather like crossing a bridge and burning it after him, tore up every scrap of paper that identified him as Bart Steele of Vega Four, graduate of the Space Academy. There were his school records filed on Earth with his fingerprints, so that he could get duplicates if he ever came back to Earth, but in effect he was wiping out five years of schooling and training. For better or worse, he was – who *was* he? He hadn't even looked at the identity papers!

He glanced at them quickly. They were made out in

the name of David Warren Briscoe, of the fourth planet of Aldebaran. According to them, he was 20 years old. He wondered, suddenly and painfully, if Briscoe had a son, and if these were his son's papers. And what would he have to say when he found out someone was using his papers?

He put the torn scraps of his old papers into the trashbin before he realised that they looked exactly like what they were: torn-up identity papers and a broken plastic ID card. *Nobody* tore up identity papers. What could he do?

Then he remembered something from the Academy. All spaceships were closed-system cycles; that meant no waste was discarded, but everything was collected in big chemical tanks, broken down into separate elements, purified and built up again into new materials. He threw the paper into the toilet, worked the plastic card back and forth, back and forth until he had wrenched it into inch-wide squares, and threw it after them.

The door of the room opened, and a Mentorian said irritably, 'Please lie down and fasten the straps, I haven't got all day.'

Hastily Bart flushed the toilet and closed the lid. 'Right away,' he said hurriedly and went to the bunk. Now his papers were on their way to the chemical breakdown tank. What was paper? Complex hydrocarbons; the hydrogen, carbon and oxygen would all be separate molecules before long. He felt like laughing hysterically at the idea that he might soon be breathing an atom of air made up of oxygen that had once been part of his identity credentials. That the very ink on his diploma might fertilize a plant in the air-purifier rooms, or the carbon of the plastic turn up as carbohydrate in synthetic food!

The Mentorian said bad-temperedly, 'You young people think the rules mean everyone but you,' and strapped him far too tightly into the bunk. For the first time, Bart felt that the general prejudice against Mentorians might make some sense after all. Just because they were the link between men and Lhari, did they have to act as if they owned everybody?

Then he made himself relax. The steward was just doing his job. An unstrapped passenger might be hurt badly in the takeoff.

The steward left, still grumbling. Bart drew a deep breath. It was the first moment he'd had to stop and think since Briscoe had grabbed him. Where was his father? Was he really doing the right thing? Or was this, somehow, a plot to keep Bart and his father apart, and was he just falling into the trap?

If he had refused, furiously, to get out of the robocab, if he had demanded that Briscoe explain, then maybe Briscoe would still be alive. And now it was too late. The grey-haired, puffing little man would never explain anything; he was now just part of a horrible puddle of melted metal. . . .

A warning siren went off in the ship, rising to hysterical intensity. Bart thought, incredulously, this is really *happening!* It felt like a nightmare. His father a fugitive from the Lhari; Briscoe dead; he himself travelling, with forged papers, to a star he'd never seen.

He braced himself, knowing that the siren was the last warning for takeoff. First there would be the hum of power, then the crushing surge of acceleration. Despite having made half a dozen trips inside the System, he still felt that moment of fear, like a bad taste in his mouth, at takeoff.

Abruptly the door opened, and Bart grabbed a fistful of bed-ticking as two Lhari came into the room. One of them said, in his shrill language, 'This boy is the right age.'

'You're seeing spies in every corner, Vorongil,'

replied the other, then addressed Bart in Universal. 'Could we trrrouble you for your papersss, sssir?'

The straps kept Bart from moving; he moved his head towards the side of the bunk, hoping his face did not betray his fear. Strapped in, helpless, he watched the two non-humans riffle through his papers with their odd claws.

'They sseem to be in orderrr,' said the Lhari. 'What isss yourr planet?'

Bart wet his lips; he had almost said 'Vega Four.'

'Aldebaran Four.'

The Lhari said in his own language, 'We should have Margil here, he saw the spies. If they had been able to stop their silly secrecy, give us the name before the dispatchers cleared the ship, we wouldn't be having this delay.'

The other replied, 'I still say he was in the machine that disintegrated. There was enough protoplasm residue for two human bodies.' Bart fought to keep his face perfectly straight.

'Did anyone come into yourr cabin?' the Lhari asked.

'Only the steward. Is something wrong?'

'Therre iss some thought that a stowaway might be on boarrd. Of courrrrse we could not allow that, anyone who did so would die in warrrpdrrrive.'

'Just the steward,' Bart said again. *Briscoe had died to give him this chance!*

The Lhari said, eyeing him keenly, 'You are ill or discommoded?'

'That – stuff the Medic made me drink,' said Bart, grasping at random for an excuse, 'made me feel – sort of sick.'

'You can send for a medical officer afterr acceleration,' said the Lhari, expressionlessly. 'The summoning bell is at yourr left, should you be in need of assistance. A pleasant trrrip to you.' They turned and

33

went out, and Bart gulped. Lhari, in person, checking the passenger decks! Normally, once you were on board, you never saw a Lhari; just Mentorians. The Lhari treated humans as too unintelligent to care about. Well, at least someone was caring enough to treat humans as worthy antagonists!

But Bart felt very alone, and scared.

A high, double-noted bell sounded. A low hum rose, somewhere in the ship, and Bart grabbed ticking as he felt the slow surge; then a violent pressure popped his eardrums, weight crowded down on him like an elephant sitting on his chest, and there was a horrible squashed sensation dragging his limbs out of shape. It grew and grew. Bart lay still and sweated, trying to ease his uncomfortable position and unable even to move a finger. The Lhari ships hit 12 gravities in the first surge of acceleration; that wasn't much, but it meant that Bart weighed twelve times his normal amount – nearly a ton! He felt as if he were spreading out, under the weight, into a puddle of flesh – *melted flesh like Briscoe's* – Bart writhed and bit his lip till he could taste blood, wishing he were young enough to bawl out loud.

Abruptly, it eased. The blood started to flow again in his numbed limbs. Bart breathed hard, loosened his straps, wiped his face – wringing wet, whether with sweat or tears he wasn't sure – and sat up in his bunk. The loudspeaker announced, 'Acceleration One is completed. Passengers on A Decks and B Decks are invited to witness the passing of the satellites from the Observation Lounge in half an hour.'

Bart got up and washed his face, remembering that he had no luggage with him – not so much as a toothbrush or a comb. He inspected the wallet Briscoe had given him. In addition to identity papers, and a planetary pilot's licence validated with four runs on the Aldebaran Interplanet Line, with the rank of Apprentice Astrogator, the wallet contained a considerable sum of money. He wouldn't starve when he got to Procyon, and when the ship's services opened, he could probably get what toilet articles he needed there.

At the back of his mind, packed up into a corner, was a sort of horror at the memory of Briscoe's death, but he put it firmly away. He might as well relax and enjoy the trip. He went down to the Observation Lounge.

It had been darkened, and one whole wall of the room was made of clear quartzite. Bart drew a deep breath as the vast panorama of space opened out before him.

They were receding from the sun at some thousands of miles a minute. Swirling past the ship, gleaming in the reflected sunlight, like iron filings moving to the motion of a magnet, were the waves of cosmic dust molecules, bright clouds around the ship. And through them, the brilliant sparkles of the fixed stars shone clear and steady; so far away that even the unthinkably rapid hurling motion of the starship could not change their position. One by one, he picked out the constellations. Aldebaran swung on the pendant chain of Taurus like a great ruby; Orion strode long-legged across the sky with a swirling nebula at his belt; Vega burned, cobalt blue, in the heart of the Lyre.

Colours, colours! Inside the atmosphere of Earth's night, the stars were all white pale sparks against black; but here against the misty-pale swirls of cosmic dust they burned with colour on colour; ruby, topaz, emerald, fire-opal, like handfuls and handfuls of burning jewels scattered on the velvet backdrop of empty space. A giant hand had flung coals and burning jewels out on the darkness, swirling them with the thin veils of colour. It was a sight Bart felt he could watch forever, and still be hungry to see; the never-changing, ever-changing colours of space. There were other passengers in the lounge, but Bart had no eyes for them. He never knew how long he stood there, dazed by the glow and glory of it.

Behind him in the darkness, after a long time, someone said softly, 'Think of being a Lhari, and not being able to see anything there but bright or brighter light! No colour at all!'

Bart came up to awareness with a shock of memory. Where he was, what he was doing, his father's danger and search – *the eighth colour!* Suddenly he felt that he could not bear to look at it any more.

A bell rang melodiously in the ship and the passengers in the lounge began to stir and move towards the door.

'I suppose that means dinner,' said the vaguely familiar voice. 'Synthetics, I suppose, but we might as well go.' The light suddenly fell on Bart's face as he moved towards the door, and the voice exclaimed, 'Bart! It can't be – is it you?'

In utter dismay, Bart looked up into the face of Tom Kendron.

In the rush of danger, he had absolutely forgotten that Tom was on the ship – he was in the one place where his careful alias was no good! Tom was regarding him with surprise, delight and wonder.

'Why ever didn't you tell me, or did you and your Dad decide at the last minute? Was that your Dad with you? I wish I'd known! Hey, it's great that we can go part way together anyhow, even if you're only going as far as Proxima – going to change there before Vega?'

Bart knew he had to cut it off somehow, quickly. In the dim light, he knew, Tom could see only his face; he stepped out under the full corridor light so that Tom could see his dark hair, and said quickly, 'Mister, you're mixing me up with somebody else!'

'Bart, come off it –' Tom's voice died out uncertainly. He blinked, and said, 'I – guess maybe – I'm sorry, I'd have sworn you were a – friend of mine.'

Bart wondered suddenly if he had done the wrong thing. At all costs he'd had to stop Tom before he said his name loudly again, but Tom was a friend – and he needed a friend. Badly.

Well, it was too late now. He stared him straight in the eye and said, 'I never saw you before in my life.'

Tom look deflated. 'Well, that *is* a coincidence. I never *saw* such a resemblance. You're even dressed about the same,' he added, shaking his head. He stepped back slightly. 'Sorry to bother you, but – are you a Vegan?'

'No.' Bart wished this were over with and he could get away before he said, or did, something that would give him away. 'Aldebaran. My name's David Briscoe.'

'Glad to meet you, Dave.' With undiscourageable friendliness, Tom stuck out his hand. 'You look a lot like a pal of mine – can't get over it,' he added, shaking his head. 'If your hair wasn't so dark, you could be his twin brother! I thought you Aldebaranians were all short and fat.... no offence meant. Say, that bell meant dinner, why don't we go down together? I don't know a soul on this ship, and it looks like luck, running into somebody who could be my best friend's twin brother!'

Bart felt warmed and drawn, but sensibly knew he could not sustain the pretence much longer. Sooner or later, he'd slip up and use some habitual phrase, some small gesture his friend would recognise.

Could he appeal to Tom – reveal his identity and ask him to keep quiet? No, this wasn't a game. One man was dead already. Tom would never purposely give him away, but he might slip up. And then they'd be in terrible danger – Tom, too. There was only one way out now. He hated to hurt Tom, but at least he wouldn't have to do it as Bart Steele. Tom could hate David Briscoe for a rude so-and-so, but he'd go on thinking of Bart Steele as his friend.

He said, coldly, 'Thank you, but I don't intend to go down to the dining room. I have other things to attend to. Perhaps we may see each other later,' and, before he could see Tom's eager friendly smile turn to hurt defensiveness, he spun around and walked away. He'd sounded like a mean, stuck-up prig. Who'd want to be friendly with a guy like that?

Back in his stateroom, he gloomily dialled himself some synthetic jellies, thinking with annoyance of the better food of the dining room. He knew he couldn't risk seeing Tom again, and drearily resigned himself to staying in his stateroom.

It looked like an awfully boring trip ahead.

It was. It was a week before the Lhari ship went into warpdrive, and all that time Bart stayed in his cabin, not daring to go to the dining hall or observation lounge. He got tired of eating synthetics, and even more tired of listening to tapes from the ship's library. But even that was better than thinking about Briscoe's fate, worrying about his father, wondering what would happen when he reached Procyon.

They had been in space a week before he finally saw another human being; he was actually relieved when a Mentorian steward came into his cabin to prepare him for coldsleep.

Bart didn't know exactly how the warpdrive worked. It had something to do with relativity; when the ship generated certain types of wave frequencies, in effect the ship went into another dimension, and came out of it again a good many light-years away. No human being had ever survived warpdrive, as far as Bart knew, except in the suspended animation called coldsleep by the Lhari scientists. While they were professionally re-assuring him and strapping him into his bunk, Bart wondered briefly what his father would do if they *did* discover the secret of the Lhari warpdrive – since humans couldn't survive it in full consciousness. Well, he supposed they could use automatic controls, or something of that sort.

The Mentorian paused, needle in hand. 'Do you want to be awakened for the week we will spend in each of the Proxima, Sirius, and Pollux systems, sir? You can, of course, be given enough drug to keep you in coldsleep until we reach the Procyon Alpha stop.'

Bart thought about that. He was terribly bored with his cabin – on the other hand, it tempted him. When he came to Earth, he hadn't seen any star systems but his own, Proxima, and Earth. There would be short stops on each of those worlds, and the cruise through their planetary systems.

Firmly, he put temptation aside. Better, after all, not to risk running into the other passengers if he got too bored with his cabin. 'I'll sleep until Procyon,' he said.

The needle went into his arm. He felt himself sinking into sleep, and in sudden panic, realized that he was now helpless. The ships would touch down on three worlds – and on any one of them, the Lhari might have his description and alias, he could be taken off the ship drugged and unconscious, he might never wake up! He tried to move, protest, tell them he had changed his mind – but already he was unable to speak. There was a sudden freezing sensation of cold. Then he was floating in what felt like coloured waves of cosmic dust; and then there was nothing, nothing at all, except the nowhere night of sleep.

And then suddenly he was cold again, and, a Mentorian face – not the same face – was bending over him, saying with soft deference, 'We have just entered the gravitational pull of Planet Alpha, Mr. Briscoe. Touchdown in three hours. How do you feel now?'

Bart's legs felt numb, when he sat up, and his hands tingled with restored circulation. But his body processes had been slowed so much by the coldsleep that he didn't even feel hungry; the synthetic jelly he'd eaten before he went to sleep (it felt like about an hour ago) hadn't even been digested yet.

With touchdown in three hours, suddenly he felt that he would stifle if he stayed in his cabin another minute. He went down to the observation lounge.

The cosmic dust was brighter out here, and the constellations had altered a little, looking flatter and more brilliant. He had travelled 47 million light years... he couldn't even calculate how many millions of miles that was. The sun was Procyon, a Sol-type star, bright yellow and very beautiful; three small planets, blue and green and gold, swung like moonstone pendants in the viewport. Past them he made out other stars, the ruby of Aldebaran....

'Your home,' said a cheery voice behind him. 'Hello, Dave. Been spacesick all this time? Remember me? I met you about six weeks ago, in the lounge, remember?'

'*Oh no!*' Bart thought, and turned to face Tom again. 'I've been in coldsleep.'

'What a dull way to face a long trip!' Tom said cheerily. 'I've been enjoying every minute of it myself. It's probably the last pleasure trip I'll take in a long time. Or have you travelled so much between the stars that you're bored with it?'

It was hard to realise that for Tom their meeting had been six weeks ago. It all seemed dreamlike anyhow. The closer he came to it, the less Bart could realise that in a few hours he would be getting off on a strange world, with no clues but the strange name Raynor Three. He felt terribly alone.

He remembered that Tom had slept for only a few hours at each warpdrive jump between stars, and spent all the planetary-travel time awake on the ship. He asked, 'How was Sirius spaceport?' and that held Tom all through dinnertime, telling about the daylong stop-over under the enormous white star, and the robocab tour he had taken of the huge spaceport – as big as a planet, almost.

'But it wasn't really much more interesting than Luna City, and when it came to sightseeing, it couldn't compare with it,' Tom added. 'In my last year at the Space Academy, four of us took the Luna City Tour. Remember the food in the Crystal Room?'

'You bet –' Bart said incautiously, then could have bitten his tongue out. Tom was regarding him with a mixture of triumph and trouble.

'Bart,' he said in a whisper. 'I was sure it was you. I was beginning to wonder, though. Why didn't you tell me, fella?'

Bart felt himself start to smile, but it only stretched his mouth. He said very low, hardly working his lips, 'Don't say my name out loud, Tom. I'm in terrible trouble.'

'Why didn't you tell me? What's a pal for?' demanded Tom indignantly.

'We can't talk here,' Bart said in an undertone, 'and all the cabins are wired for sound, in case somebody stops breathing or has a heart attack in space. Where can we go?'

They stood at the very edge of the quartz window, seeming to hang on the brink of a dizzying gulf of cosmic space, and talked in whispers, while Procyon Alpha, Beta and Gamma swelled like blown-up balloons in the viewport. Tom heard his story, almost incredulous.

'And your father's disappeared? Listen, though, Bart,' Tom said, 'The Lhari checked my room, too, and asked questions at all the ports. I wondered why. It must have been my Space Academy papers, so they probably already know you aren't on Earth. If they follow you, you might even lead them to your father!'

'I honestly don't think so,' Bart said slowly. 'I don't

41

think Briscoe even knew where Dad was.'

'Then how can you be sure of finding him?' Tom urged. 'You'd better come to Capella with me. You can stay with my family, and appeal to the Interplanet Authority to find your father. They'd protect him against the Lhari, wouldn't they?'

'Briscoe was afraid –'

'Briscoe sounds like a thoroughly shady character,' Tom said firmly. 'How do you know he came from your father? This whole Raynor Three business might be a trap.'

It appealed to Bart – the idea of going on with Tom, feeling safe again. Letting the Interplanet Authority handle it. Why, if they'd done that on Earth, Briscoe would be alive now.

'That's the sensible thing,' Tom argued. 'You can't run around playing interplanetary spy all by yourself!'

But Briscoe had died – deliberately gone to his own death, to give Bart a chance to get away. He wouldn't have done that just to send Bart into a trap. And there had been the message of the eighth colour.

'Thanks, Tom,' Bart said slowly, 'but I'll have to play it my way.'

Tom hesitated, then said firmly, 'Count me in, then! My ticket has stop-over privileges. I'll get off at Procyon with you, and if anything happens to you, I'll go straight to the Port Authority for Procyon, and make sure the Lhari have to account for your safety!'

It was a temptation! To have a friend at his back – then he remembered, with fresh horror, the ugly puddle of the melted robocab and Briscoe; the Lhari had said callously, 'Protoplasm residue enough for two bodies.' He couldn't let Tom face that. It was his own danger.

'I appreciate that,' he said, 'but they've looked awfully close at you already, Tom. If we team up, they're sure to suspect there is some connection. You'd only make the danger worse. The best thing you can do is to stay out of it.'

The three planets grew and grew in the viewport. Bart was almost relieved when a warning bell rang in the ship and he broke sharply away from Tom with a curt 'Be careful,' and went to his cabin, to be strapped in for the surge of deceleration.

He went through another decontamination chamber, and finally stepped out under the strange sun, into the strange world.

At first sight it was a disappointment. It was a Lhari spaceport, identical with the one on Earth, or so it seemed; full of sloping glass ramps, moving stairways, high glass pylons. But the sun overhead was brilliant and clear gold, and the shadows sharp and violet. The air had a strange warm salty smell. Beyond the confines of the spaceport he could see the ridges of tall hills and unfamiliar colours of trees, but he got a grip on his imagination and surrendered his ticket stub and papers to the Lhari guard and Mentorian interpreter.

The Lhari said briefly in his own language to the Mentorian, 'Keep him for questioning, but don't tell him why.' Bart felt a cold chill going up and down his spine. *This was it* –

The Mentorian said idly, 'We wish to check the luggage of all Aldebaranians. There will be a brief delay of about thirty minutes. Will you kindly wait in that room there?' He gestured towards a doorway.

The room was comfortable, furnished with chairs and a visionscreen with some colourful story moving on it. Small bright figures in capes, curious beasts racing across an unusual veldt, but Bart paced the room restlessly. There were two doors in the room, the one through which he had come – and another. But this one was marked clearly DANGER. HUMANS MUST NOT PASS WITHOUT SPECIAL LENSES.

43

BEYOND THIS POINT THERE IS DANGER OF BLINDNESS TO HUMAN EYES. Below it, in special letters, was a smaller warning: *Ordinary dark glasses are not safe: Lhari lights!* That was no way out, Bart thought.

Maybe his papers would stand a routine check, but he felt a terrible nervousness and unease.

He paced the room restlessly, looking at the door and the warning. He had heard that the Lhari sun was almost five hundred times as bright as Earth's sun, a hundred times brighter than Vega. Only the Mentorians could endure Lhari lights –

A sudden, desperate plan occurred to Bart. He knew he might be blinded at once; he didn't know just how much light he could tolerate – he'd never been under a star with that much brilliance. But he knew he had inherited some of his mother's tolerance for light, and blindness was less of a risk than being melted down with an energon-gun, anyhow! He went hesitantly towards the door, and pushed it open.

His eyes exploded in pain, and automatically his hands went up to shield them. Light, light – he had never known such cruel glowing light, it seemed to dim out all sight. His eyes, outraged, dripped red and yellow after-images; but after a moment, squeezing his eyes shut and opening them a slit, he found he could see. He shoved the door shut and made out, through the glare, other doors, glass ramps, small offices with glass walls and floors and colourless furniture. He was standing near one of the office doors, and one of the silky metallic cloaks worn by Mentorians doing spaceport work was hanging on a peg. On an impulse, Bart caught it up and flung it around his shoulders.

It felt cool and soft, and the hood shielded his eyes a little from the glare. The ramp leading down to what he hoped was street level was terribly steep, and there were no steps. Bart was not used to Lhari buildings or their furnishings, but he had done plenty of acrobatics at the Space Academy. He eased himself over the top of the ramp and let go. He whooshed down the slick surface on the flat of his back, feeling the metal of the cloak heating rapidly, and came to a breathless stop at the bottom. *Whew, what a slide! Three storeys, at least!* But there was a door, and maybe, outside the door, was safety –

A voice hailed him, in the shrill Lhari speech.

'Where are you going? You there, you should have glasses on, your eyes will be permanently damaged!'

Bart made out, in the cruel glare, the form of a Lhari, only a colourless blob in the light, with a gold cloak and the jagged insignia on the front of high tights. 'You people know better than to come back here,' the Lhari said in his high whistling voice. 'Do you think we would like to have you blinded, my friend?' He actually sounded concerned.

So they called the Mentorian *friends* in that condescending way? Bart tensed, but his heart pounded. Now he was fairly caught; could he bluff his way out? He hadn't spoken a word of the Lhari language in years and years, though his mother had taught it to him when he was a child.

Well, he must try . . .

He might as well make a good lie of it!

'Margil sent me back to check, and see if anyone escaped this way,' he tweetled as best he could. 'They're looking for a prisoner who seems to have escaped when he was being held for questioning. I came in a hurry.'

The Lhari regarded him curiously through those slitted eyes, and said, 'So that creature has slipped through their fingers again? What is the *matter*, that one man can give us the slip this way? Well, one thing is sure, he couldn't come this way without being blinded – he's from Vega or Aldebaran, one of the dim stars. If he does come this way, we'll catch him easily enough while he's stumbling around blind. And you shouldn't try it, you know. Go on – go out this way,' he gestured, 'and go around and come in the ordinary way – but get your glasses first!'

Bart nodded, jerking the cloak about his shoulders, forcing himself not to break into a run as he stepped through the door the Lhari held for him.

It closed behind him. Bart blinked, feeling as if he were suddenly in pitch darkness; only slowly did he become aware that he was standing in a city street, in the full glare of Procyon sunlight, and he was outside a closed blank door and outside the Lhari spaceport entirely.

He'd better take cover quickly! He took off the Mentorian cloak, started to fling it away, then rolled it up under his arm; if they found it, they'd guess, and it might be useful again. He raised his eyes and stopped dead.

Just across the street was a long, low, rainbow-coloured building. And the letters – Bart couldn't believe his eyes – spelled out:

EIGHT   COLOURS   PLANETARY   TRADE
CORPORATION
CARGO, PASSENGERS, MESSAGES, EXPRESS
A. RAYNOR ONE, PROPRIETOR.

Chapter Four

For a moment the words swirled before Bart's dizzied eyes. He wiped them, trying to steady himself. *Eight Colours!* Had he so soon reached the end of his dangerous quest? Was this, indeed, the safe place where he could avoid the vigilance of the Lhari? Briscoe had told him, but somehow he had expected it to be in deep, dark concealment. He read the sign again. There it was, right out in the open: EIGHT COLOURS.

Raynor One. The existence of a Raynor *one* presupposed a Raynor *two*, and probably a Raynor *three* – for all he knew, Raynors four, five and fifty-five! It couldn't be coincidence. The building looked solid and real. It was even a little shabby; it had been there a long time, though the neon sign might have been new.

With his hand on the door, he hesitated, a last-minute panic touching him. Was it, after all, the *right* Eight Colours? But it was a family saying; hardly the kind of expression you'd be apt to hear. And would Briscoe have died to send him into a trap? He pushed the door and went in.

The room was chrome and glass, filled with brighter light than the Procyon sun outdoors, the edges of the furniture rimmed with shimmering neon in the Mentorian style. A prim-looking girl sat behind a desk – or what should have been a desk, except that it looked more like a mirror with little sparkles of lights, different colours, in regular rows along one edge. The mirror-top itself was blue violet, and gave her skin and her violet eyes an odd bluish tinge; she was smooth and lacquered and glittering, and she raised her eyebrows at Bart in his Earth clothes as if he were some strange form of life she hadn't seen very often.

'Have you an appointment?'

He wondered what would happen if he asked for Rupert Steele – or for Raynor Three. Instead he said, 'I'd like to see Raynor One, if I may.'

Her dainty pointed fingernail, varnished blue, stabbed at points of light. 'On what business?' she asked, not caring.

'It's a personal matter.'

'Then I suggest you see him at his home.'

'I don't know where his home is,' Bart said, 'and it's important.'

The girl studied the glassy surface and punched at some more of the little lights. A little visionscreen cleared, but she bent over it so that Bart could not see. Her fingers moved swiftly and at last she said, 'What is your name, please?'

He wondered what would happen if he gave his real name. But at the last minute he didn't. The girl was a Mentorian, after all, and they sometimes worked with the Lhari.

'David Briscoe.'

He had thought her perfect-painted face could not show any emotion except disdain, but now it did. She looked up at him in open, blank consternation. She said into the visionscreen, 'He calls himself David Briscoe. Yes, I know. Yes, sir, yes.' She raised her face; it was controlled again, but not bored. 'Raynor One will see you. Go through that door and down to the end of the hall.'

Bart pushed the door aside. The lights here were

almost Mentorian in intensity, but his eyes were getting used to it again. His head ached, though. He'd been on Earth too long. It would take him a couple of days to get used to Vega, even!

At the end of the hallway was another door. He stepped through into a small cubicle, and the door slid quickly shut after him. He whirled in panic, then subsided in foolish relief as the cubicle began to rise; it was just an automatic lift.

Higher and higher it rose, stopping with an abruptness that gave Bart a sinking sensation in his stomach, and slid open into a lighted room and office. In the office a man sat behind a desk – a plain, ordinary desk this time – watching Bart step from the lift.

The man was very tall and thin, and some indefinable look in the grey eyes, as well as the very bright lights, told Bart that the man was a Mentorian. A small sign over the door said RAYNOR ONE, MANAGER. Raynor One regarded Bart with a steady grey stare, stern, almost grim, as Bart stepped out of the lift, and Bart felt his heart pound with a slow, clutching grab and suck of panic. Was this man a slave of the Lhari, who would turn him over to them? Or – Bart's own mother was a Mentorian; was this man someone he could trust?

'Who are you?' Raynor One asked. His voice was harsh and – not loud, but it gave an impression of being loud.

'David Briscoe,' said Bart. It was the wrong thing. Raynor One's lips went tight and forbidding.

'Try again. I happen to know that David Briscoe is dead.'

Bart began to take out his papers; with an impatient gesture, Raynor One waved them away. 'I'll admit you have papers in any name you choose,' he said. 'What I want to know is how.'

Bart hesitated. He said, 'I was given these papers with

a message for Raynor Three.'

Raynor kept on staring with those cold bright eyes. 'That is very interesting,' he said slowly. 'So it's Three you want? What is your business with him?'

On a sudden inspiration, Bart said, 'I'll tell you that if you can tell me what the eighth colour is.'

There was a glint in Raynor One's eyes now, but the even, stern voice did not soften. 'I never knew, myself. I didn't name it Eight Colours. Maybe it's the other owner you want.'

On a suddener hope, Bart asked, 'Was he, by any chance, named Rupert Steele?'

Raynor One made a suspicious movement. 'I can't imagine why you think so,' he said guardedly. 'Especially if you've just come in from Earth. It was never very widely known. He only changed the name to Eight Colours a few weeks ago. And it's for sure that your ship didn't get any messages while the Lhari were in warpdrive. You mention entirely too many names, but I notice you aren't giving out any further information.'

'I'm looking for a man called Rupert Steele –'

'I thought you were looking for Raynor Three,' said Raynor One, staring at the Mentorian cloak. 'I can think of a lot of people who might want to know how I react to certain names, and find out if I know the wrong people, if they are the wrong people. What makes you think I'd admit it, if I did?'

Now, Bart thought, they had reached a deadlock. Somebody had to trust somebody. This could go on all night – parry and riposte, question and evasive answer, each of them throwing back the other's questions in a verbal fencing match. It was certain that Raynor One wasn't giving away any information. And, considering what was probably at stake, Bart didn't blame him much.

He flung the Mentorian cloak down on the table.

'This got me out of trouble – the hard way,' he said. 'I never wore one before and I never intend to again! I want to find Rupert Steele because he's my father!'

'Your father,' Raynor One repeated. 'And just how are you going to prove that exceptionally interesting statement?'

Quite suddenly, Bart lost his temper.

'Between you and me, I don't care whether I prove it or not! You sit there, calm and quiet, giving nice, safe, foxy answers to everything I say, and expect me to do all the proving! You try proving something for a change, why don't you? If you know Rupert Steele, I don't have to prove who I am – just take a good look at me! I'm supposed to look like him – or so Briscoe told me. A man named Briscoe – a man who called himself Briscoe, anyhow! *He* gave me these papers!' Bart struck them, hard, on the desk, bending over Raynor One angrily. 'I didn't ask for them, I didn't want them; he shoved them into my hand. *That* Briscoe is dead. The Lhari shot him down in a robocab.' He felt his face twitch. He was never to be wholly free of the memory.

'He sent me here and told me to find a man named Raynor Three. But the only one I'm interested in finding is my father. Now you know as much as I do! How about giving me some information for a change? Or shall I head for the Port Authorities instead?'

He ran out of breath and stood, fists clenched, glaring down at Raynor One. Raynor One got up and said, quick, savage and quiet, 'Did anyone see you come in here?'

'Only the girl downstairs,' Bart said.

'You're in luck, maybe,' said Raynor One in a grim voice. 'How did you get through the Lhari? In that?' He moved his head at the Mentorian cloak.

Bart explained briefly, and Raynor One shook his head.

'You were lucky,' he said, 'you could have been

blinded. You must have inherited flash-accommodation as a completely dominant trait from the Mentorian side – Rupert Steele didn't have it. I'll tell you this much,' he added, sitting down again, 'since in a manner of speaking you're my boss. Eight Colours – it used to be Alpha Trans-shipping Corporation – is what they call a middleman outfit. The various interplanet shipping lines transport cargo from planet to planet within a star system – that's free competition – and the Lhari ships transport from star to star: that's a complete monopoly all over the Galaxy. Well, the middleman outfits arrange for orderly and businesslike trans-shipping between the two kinds of outfits. The Lhari prefer to deal with Mentorians, anyway. Well, Rupert Steele bought into this company a long time ago. He left it, pretty much, for me to manage; he stayed on Vega, and ran Vega Interplanet. Until a little while ago.' Raynor leaned over and punched a button. 'Violet, get Three for me,' he said into the intercom. 'You may have to send a message to the *Multiphase*. Be careful.'

Bart waited, and Raynor swung round to him.

'You want a lot of explanations,' he said. 'Well, you'll have to get 'em from somebody else. I don't know what this business is all about. I don't *want* to know. I have to do business with the Lhari – which doesn't mean I have to tell them all I know. But everything's in a mess lately, we're all hung up on trans-shipping, while the Lhari inspect cargo – costs have doubled. The less I know, the less I'm apt to say to the wrong people. But I promised Three that if you showed up, or if anyone came and asked me for the eighth colour, I'd send you to him. So don't tell me anything. I don't want to know. It's not good business for me to know things.'

He sounded mad. He motioned Bart ungraciously to a seat. 'I don't want to ask you any questions and I don't want any answers. I just wanted to make sure you weren't going to make any trouble for Three, that's all.'

He shut his mouth determinedly, as if he had already said too much. Bart sat there. After a while he heard the whine of a lift again; the panel slid open and a second man came into the room.

Bart guessed, even before he spoke, that this was Raynor Three. For he was as like Raynor One as Tweedledum to Tweedledee, although he wore the full uniform of a Mentorian on the Lhari ships; the white smock and Medical insignia, the metallic cloak and tights, the low silvery sandals. Raynor Three said, 'Your message just caught me on the ship, One; I was leaving for the country. What is it this time?'

'Steele's youngster,' said Raynor One expressionlessly.

And here for the first time Bart saw the difference in the – were they brothers? Twins? Two of triplets? For Raynor One had not altered his stern, controlled, grim face all through their interview; but as he spoke the name, Raynor Three's eyes narrowed and he drew a quick breath, his face twisting up into apprehension and shock. Raynor Three turned to look at Bart.

'It's young Steele, right enough,' he said, his voice dropping to gentleness. 'Did he come in on his own name? How'd he manage it?'

'No. He had David Briscoe's papers. Evidently the old man got them through.'

'The crazy fool,' said Raynor Three, with a quick intake of breath, and turned to Bart. 'Quick, give them to me, Bart.'

Bart hesitated. Raynor One walked to the window and said in his deadpan voice, 'It's really useless. You'll never get anywhere, Three. But get the kid out of here before they come looking for me. Look down there.'

He pointed. Down below them there was a scramble in the streets; Lhari fanning out in all directions, uniformed guards, Mentorians, Bart turned sick.

'They're sure to look here,' Raynor One said. 'They must have checked their messaging service. If they had the same efficiency with red tape that we humans have, young Steele wouldn't have made it this far. Fortunately they only had one description, and then the wrong name. Now they may have both.'

Raynor Three nodded. 'It's the old double-shuffle trick,' he said to Bart. 'They had Steele's description but not his name – so Briscoe managed to take Steele's papers and slip through with them. Once they landed on Earth, and got their messages cleared, they had the Steele names – both of them – but by that time Briscoe had slipped through their fingers, I suppose –'

'No, he's dead,' Bart said harshly, 'the Lhari killed him.'

Raynor Three's mobile face displayed shock and sadness. But he went on, ' – by that time, you were outbound with *another* set of papers. It may have confused them because they knew that *David* Briscoe was dead, and there was a chance you might be an innocent bystander who could raise a real row if they pulled you in. But the name Briscoe is known here. You aren't safe – we'll have to destroy these.'

He touched the set of false papers lightly with a finger.

'Two brave men,' he said softly. 'Edmund Briscoe the father, David Briscoe the son. Remember the name, Bart, because I won't remember it.'

'Why not?'

Raynor Three gave him a gold-glinting, enigmatic glance and said, 'I'm a Mentorian, remember? I work for the Lhari. My stock in trade is *not* remembering things. Just be glad I remember Rupert Steele. If you'd been a few days later, I wouldn't have remembered him, though I promised to wait for you.'

It was all very confusing, but before Bart could

demand any more explanations, Raynor One broke in, 'Get him *out* of here! They're coming!'

Raynor Three swung to Bart, saying nervously, 'Can you speak the Lhari language?'

Bart nodded.

'Put that on, then.' He gestured to the Mentorian cloak. 'That's right – pull the hood right up over your head,' he added, as Bart obeyed, 'and if we meet anyone, say a polite good afternoon in Lhari, and leave the rest of the talking to me.' He thrust the Briscoe identity papers into a disposal chute. Bart watched them go in apprehension and regret. Now he had neither his own nor a forged identity, and it dismayed him.

They went down in the elevator into the street that was full of Lhari. No one paid any attention to Raynor Three and Bart, in the metallic cloaks, but Raynor Three whispered, 'Attack is the best defence,' and went up to one of the Lhari.

'What's going on?'

'A passenger on the ship got away without going through Decontam,' the Lhari said. 'He may spread disease on the planet, so of course we have alerted all authorities.'

Raynor Three turned around to Bart and said clearly, 'Hear that? We'll keep an eye out for him.'

As the Lhari vanished, Raynor Three's expressive face twisted into a grimace. 'Really clever, that. So that's the story! Now the whole planet will be alive with people looking for any stranger, crazy with fear lest you bring some unauthorized germs along! We'd better get you to a safe place.'

'Shall I call a robocab?'

Raynor Three chuckled. 'No, on this planet we're allowed to own private transportation. I have a copter of my own. Good thing, too; public cabs have records.'

Bart demanded, as they climbed in, 'Are you taking

me to my father?'

'Wait till we get to my place,' Raynor Three said, taking the controls and putting the machine in the air. 'Just lean back and enjoy the trip, huh?' He applied himself to the controls.

Bart relaxed against the cushions, but he still felt apprehensive. Too much had happened too fast. He wished he could get a message to Tom, but knew no way to do it.

Where was his father? Was Raynor Three taking him to his father? He told himself, sternly, that if his father was a fugitive from the Lhari, he might very well have moved on and by now be at the other end of the Galaxy. But if his father couldn't travel on Lhari ships, and if he had been here, then the chances were that he was still on this world. Or somewhere, at least, in the Procyon system.

They flew for a long time, across a quiet countryside of low hills, patchwork agricultural districts, two or three towns and cities, and then for a long time over water. Bart noticed that the copter had an automatic control setting, but Raynor Three kept it on manual, and Bart wondered if the Mentorian just didn't want to talk. Anyway, he trusted Raynor Three, without knowing why.

The copter began to come down, at last, towards a small yellow-green hill, bright in the last gold rays of the sun. A small dome-like green bubble rose out of the hill; it opened smoothly. Raynor Three set the copter neatly down on a small platform that slid shut after them, unfastened their seat belts, and gave Bart a hand to climb out. He clicked on lights, slid a panel aside, and ushered Bart into a living room of glass and chrome, pleasant, softly lighted, but deserted and faintly dusty. Raynor pushed a switch; soft music came on, and the carpets caressed his feet.

He motioned Bart to a soft chair.

'Well, you're safe here for a while,' Raynor Three said, 'though how long it will last, nobody knows. So far I've been above suspicion.'

It seemed a queer phrase to use. How did he manage to escape the probing, or brainwashing, given to all Mentorians who worked for the Lhari? And what was his connection with all this? Bart leaned back; the chair was very comfortable, but it did not wholly disarm his suspicions.

'Where is my father?'

Raynor Three stood looking down at him, his mobile face drawn and strange, his mouth twisted painfully. He said at last, 'I guess I can't put it off any longer. I'd hoped –' he broke off. 'I have his things here, Bart. I'll give them to you.'

The words seemed to say more than they had actually said. Apprehension tightened its fist around Bart's throat; he could hardly speak.

'Where is he?' he demanded. 'Where's Dad? What's wrong?'

Raynor Three covered his face with his hands. From behind them hoarse words came, choked with emotion.

'Your father is dead, Bart. I – I killed him.'

Chapter Five

For a moment Bart stared, frozen, unable to move, his very ears refusing the words he heard. Had this all been another cruel trick, then, a trap, a betrayal? He rose and looked wildly around the room, as if the glass walls were a cage closing in on him.

'Murderer!' he flung at Raynor, and took a step towards him, his clenched fists coming up. He'd been shoved around too long, but here he had one of them right in front of him, and for once he'd hit back! He'd start by taking Raynor Three apart – in small pieces! His rage and grief boiled over, all the worse because he had so instinctively liked and trusted this man. 'You – you rotten murderer!'

Raynor Three looked at him, his face wrung, but made no move to defend himself. 'Bart,' he said compassionately, 'sit down and listen to me. No, I'm no murderer. I – I shouldn't have put it that way –'

Bart's hands dropped to his sides, but he heard his voice crack with pain and grief.

'I suppose you'll tell me he was a spy or a traitor and you *had* to kill him! You – you *slave* of the Lhari!'

'Not even that,' Raynor Three said. 'And I tried hard to save him, Bart. I did everything I could, I'm no murderer. I killed him yes – God forgive me, because I'll never forgive myself! But when you know –' The grief in his face could not be doubted or questioned. Bart's fists

58

unclenched, and he stared down at Raynor Three, shaking his head in bewilderment and grief. The words burst from him like sobs.

'I knew he was dead, all along! I was – trying not to believe it, but I knew!'

Raynor bowed his head. 'I wish I hadn't had to be the one to tell you. I liked your father, Bart; I admired him. He took a long chance, and it killed him. But I should have stopped him. If anyone could have stopped him.'

'If only I'd been here!' Bart cried out.

Slowly, Raynor Three shook his head. 'It would have happened just the same, even if you'd been here,' he said. But Bart was not listening. He bent in his chair, his face in his hands, his whole being in revolt and shock.

Dad, oh Dad! I kept going because I thought, at the end of it all, you'd be there, and it would be all over. But here I am, and you're not here, you won't ever be here again! Dimly, he knew that Raynor Three rose and quietly left the room, leaving him alone; he put his head in his arms, giving way to his grief and shock, and cried.

After a while he raised his head and blew his nose, feeling his face setting itself in new, hard, unaccustomed lines, slowly coming to terms with the hard, painful reality. His father was dead. His dangerous, dead-in-earnest game of escape had no happy ending in reunion with his father. They couldn't sit together and laugh about how scared he had been. His father was *dead* – and he, Bart, was alone and in danger. His face looked very grim indeed, and years older than he was.

After a long time Raynor Three opened the door quietly and said, 'Come and have something to eat, Bart.'

'I'm not hungry.'

'Well, I am,' Raynor Three said, 'and you ought to be. Come on, don't be childish. You'll need it.' He pulled knobs and the appropriate tables and chairs extruded themselves from the walls; Raynor unsealed hot cartons and spread them on the table, saying lightly, 'Looks good – not that I can claim any credit; I subscribe to a food service that delivers them hot by pneumatic tube.'

Bart felt sickened by the thought of eating, but when he put a polite fork in the food, he discovered that he was famished – after weeks in space, living on synthetics – and ate up everything in sight. When they had finished, Raynor dumped the cartons into a disposal chute, went to a small portable bar and put a glass into his hand.

'Drink this.'

Bart touched his lips to the glass, made a face and put it away. 'Thanks, but I don't drink.'

'Call it medicine, you'll need something,' Raynor Three said crossly. 'I've got a lot to tell you, and I don't want you going off half-primed in the middle of a sentence. If you'd rather have a shot of tranquilliser, all right, otherwise, I prescribe that you drink what I gave you.' He gave Bart a quick, wry grin. 'I really am a Medic, you know.'

Feeling childish and awkward about his protest, Bart drank. It burned his mouth, but after it was down, he felt a sort of warm burning in his insides that spread a sort of glow and sense of well-being over him. It wasn't alcohol, but whatever it was, it had quite a kick to it! He realised he was being treated with great kindness.

'Feel better?'

Bart muttered, 'Thanks.'

After a minute he asked, 'Why are you taking all this trouble, Raynor? There must be some danger –'

'Why, don't you –' Raynor broke off. 'That's right,' he said, 'you were brought up a Vegan; I don't suppose your mother ever went very deeply into your Mentorian family tree. You were so young when she died. Her father was a Raynor – Twelve, to be exact.'

He smiled again at Bart, a little ruefully. 'I won't claim any of the privileges of a kinsman until you decide how much to trust me,' he said.

'Look, I – I was sort of in shock,' Bart said.

Raynor Three settled back, a drink in his hand.

'It's a long story,' he began, 'and I only know part of it. Maybe you'll find out, or fill in, the rest of it yourself.

'I'm a Mentorian. Our family, the Raynors, have traded with the Lhari for generations, but that doesn't mean that we necessarily believe the Lhari treaty is right, or just. When I was a young man, I qualified as a Medic on the Lhari ships, and I've been starhopping ever since. People call me a slave of the Lhari – maybe we are, maybe all the Mentorians are,' he added wryly. 'But I travel on the Lhari ships simply because space is where I belong, and there's no place else that I want to be. And that's the only way I can have it – so I take it. Even if it means losing my memory, more or less, every few years.

'I never questioned what I was doing until a few years ago, when I met your father. He made me realise that we Mentorians were being blind and selfish. This privilege ought to belong to everyone, not just to the Lhari. More and more, the Lhari monopoly began to seem unfair to me. But it didn't seem there was anything I could do to fight it. I was just a Medic. And if I got involved with any conspiracy against the Lhari, they'd find it out when they did the routine psych-checking, and I'd lose my place on the Lhari ships. I'd be planet-bound again.

'And then we worked out how to do it. Before every trip, with self-hypnosis and suggestion, I erase my own memories – a sort of artificial amnesia – so that the Lhari can't find out any more than I want them to find out. And after every trip – my brother One keeps my records – I go back and listen to my own tapes and find out what I knew before.

'So far, it was just an impalpable sort of group, trying to put together stray bits of information that the Lhari didn't think important enough to censor from their Mentorians.

'And then came the big breakthrough. There was a young apprentice astrogator named David Briscoe. He'd taken some runs in special test ships, and read some extremely obscure research data from the early days of the contact between men and Lhari, and he had a wild idea. He did the bravest thing anyone has ever done. He stripped himself of all identifying data – so if he died, no one would be in trouble with the Lhari – and stowed away on a Lhari ship.'

'But –' Bart's lips were dry, 'didn't he die in the warpdrive?'

Slowly, Raynor Three shook his head.

'No, he didn't. No drugs, no coldsleep – but he didn't die. Don't you see, Bart?' He leaned forward, urgently.

'*It's all a fake!* The Lhari have just been saying that – to justify their refusal to give us the secret of the catalyst that generates the warpdrive frequencies! Such a simple lie, and it's worked for all those years!

'Young Briscoe managed to get off the Lhari ship – a Mentorian found him and didn't have the heart to turn him over to the Lhari. So he was smuggled clear again. But when that Mentorian underwent the routine brain-checks at the end of the voyage, the Lhari found out what had happened. They didn't know Briscoe's name, but they wrung that Mentorian out like a wet dishcloth and got a description that was as good as fingerprints. They tracked down Briscoe – young Briscoe – and killed him. They killed the first man he'd talked to. They killed the second. The third was your father.'

Bart was shaking, sick with hate. 'The murdering devils!'

Slowly, Raynor Three shook his head. 'No,' he said. 'I don't expect you to understand, though. Anyway, your father and Briscoe's father were old friends. Rupert Steele knew that everyone he talked to was doomed; the Lhari had traced young Briscoe's movements. Briscoe's father was dying with an incurable heart disease. *His* son was dead, and old Briscoe had only one thought in his mind: to make sure he didn't die for nothing. Your father didn't dare come to Earth and get you, Bart, he knew he'd be followed wherever he went. So old Briscoe took your father's papers, knowing they were as good as a death-warrant, slipped away, and got on a Lhari ship that led roundabout to stars where the message hadn't reached yet. He led them a good chase. Did he die, or did they track him down and kill him?'

Bart bowed his head and told the story in a choked voice. Briscoe had actually *goaded* the Lhari to shoot him down. *But he'd got one of them. . . .*

'Meanwhile,' Raynor Three continued, 'your father came to me, knowing I was sympathetic and knowing I was a Lhari-trained surgeon. He had just one thought in his mind; to do, again, what Briscoe had done, and make sure the news got out. He sent out messages, in code, all over the Galaxy – Eight Colours handled that. And then he cooked up a plan that was even braver, and more desperate, than what young David Briscoe had done. He decided to sign on a Lhari ship – as a member of the crew.'

'As a Mentorian?' Bart asked, but something cold, like icewater trickling down his back, told him this was not what Raynor meant. 'The brainwashing...'

'No,' said Raynor quietly. 'Not as a Mentorian. *As a Lhari.*'

Bart gasped. 'How – ?'

'Men and Lhari are very much alike,' Raynor Three

said. 'A few small things – the shape of the ears, the hands – keep humans from seeing that the Lhari are men –'

'Don't say that!' Bart almost yelled. 'Those rotten, filthy, murdering *devils* – those monsters – men?'

'Do you want that tranquillising shot?' Raynor asked drily. 'I've lived among the Lhari all my life. They're not Devils with a big D, Bart, they're just people, trying to live the best way they can.'

'And you Mentorians are as bad as they are!' Bart flung at him. He rose and paced around the room, angrily. Raynor watched him with a sigh, finally saying, 'They're not violent people really. Forget that for a moment; we can argue politics later. If you knew what the Lhari were trying to do –'

'*Dad knew!*'

'Bart, I'm on your side,' Raynor reminded him. 'The point is this. Physiologically, the Lharis are humanoid. They're a whole lot more like men than a man is like, for instance, a gorilla. *Homo Lharis* is more like *homo sapiens* than either is like a Neanderthal man for that matter. By minor facial and plastic surgery, he convinced me he could pass as a Lhari, and finally I gave in, and did the surgery. . . .'

'And it killed him!' Bart burst out.

Raynor sighed. 'Not really. The risks were almost negligible. It was really a completely unforeseen accident; a blood clot broke loose from one of the most minor incisions and lodged in his brain. He was dead in seconds, and by the time I could get the heart action started again, it was too late. It could have happened at any time,' he said, but his face twisted. 'I feel responsible, even though I keep telling myself I'm not.

'And now, I've done everything I can do, Bart. I can get you forged credentials, and change your appearance just enough so that the Lhari can't catch you. I'll do that for your father's sake – and your mother's. I won't remember this, you know. The Lhari don't watch me too closely; they figure that anything I do, they'll catch in the brainwashing. Whereas Raynor One is watched all the time, since he's not subject to their psych-checking. But I'm still one step ahead of them, as long as I can erase my own memories. But you'll have to do something for us. It's not dangerous, but you'll have to tell them your father is dead and the plan failed.' He sank back, with a sigh, mixed himself a fresh drink, and drank it all.

Bart was sifting it all, slowly, in his mind. At last he said, 'Why was Dad doing this? What could he hope to gain?'

Raynor Three said, 'You know that we can build ships just like the Lhari ships. But we don't know anything about the rare catalyst they use for fuel. Captain Steele had hopes of being able to discover where they got it.'

'But couldn't they find out where the Lhari ships go for fuelling?'

Raynor shook his head. 'No. there's no way to trail a Lhari ship,' he reminded Bart. 'We can follow them inside a star system but then they pop into warpdrive, and only the Lhari themselves know where they come out. Oh, we know what their regular runs are between the human-inhabited star systems, of course. Those coordinates are common knowledge. But we don't know where they go when they aren't running between *our* stars.

'We've gathered together what information we *do* have, and we know that after a certain number of runs in our part of the Galaxy, ships take off in the direction of Antares. There's a ship, due to come in here in about ten days, called the *Swiftwing*, which is just about due to make the Antares run. Captain Steele had managed to arrange – I don't know how, and I don't want to know how – for a vacancy on that ship, and somehow he got credentials. You see, it's a very good spy system, a network between the stars – but the weak link is this: everything, every message, every man, has to travel back and forth by the Lhari ships themselves.'

He rose, shaking it all off impatiently. 'Well, it's finished now. Your father is dead. What are you going to do? If you want to go back to Vega, you can probably convince the Lhari you're just an innocent bystander. They *don't* hurt bystanders or children, Bart. They aren't bad people. They're just protecting their business monopoly. I can even erase your memories of what I've told you tonight; then you can let the Lhari capture you; they won't kill you, they'll just give you a routine psych-check. Illegal, but harmless. When they find out you don't know anything, they'll send you back to Vega, and you can spend your life running your own Interplanet company very comfortably. You're a rich man, remember, Bart.'

Bart got up and swung on him. 'You mean I should just go home like a good little boy and pretend none of this ever happened? What kind of – of duffer do you think I am?'

Raynor smiled, an unexpected sweet smile that made his face very kind. 'I'd hoped you'd say that.'

'I'm going on where Dad left off,' Bart said, and his chin set in the new, hard line.

'There is a little danger involved, then,' Raynor said. 'Go as a passenger to Antares – I can get you some papers, and change your appearance just a little, and you get in touch with the man who was going to contact your father. You'll have to go on the *Swiftwing*; they'll be expecting him to travel on that ship, and the *Swiftwing* will be on Antares before a message could reach them any other way.'

Bart sprang up. 'No,' he said, 'I know a better way, Raynor! Let me go in my father's place – *as a Lhari!*'

Raynor Three's gold-glinted eyes surveyed him with an odd questioning look, but he said flatly, 'It's too dangerous. You'd never get away with it.'

Chapter Six

'All right, Bart, today we'll let you look at yourself,' Raynor Three said.

Bart felt himself smile under the muffling layers of bandages around his face. His hands were bandaged too, and his head, and he had not been permitted to look in a mirror.

The transition had been surprisingly painless – or perhaps his sense of well-being had been due to Raynor slipping him some drug; he wasn't sure. He'd been taking so many pills, morning, noon, and night, that he'd lost count.

The chief change had been that he'd been given injections of a drug that would change the colour of his skin. He would have to keep taking it regularly while his disguise lasted. There had been minor operations on his face, his hands and his feet.

'Let's see you get up and walk around,' Raynor Three said. Bart obeyed, awkwardly, and Raynor frowned. 'Hurt?'

'Not exactly, it's just that I feel as if I were limping.'

'That's natural,' Raynor said. 'I made a small change in the angle of the heel tension and the muscle of the arch. You're using a different set of muscles when you walk; until they harden up, you'll have some charley horses, but you'll get used to that. Have any trouble hearing me?'

'No, though I'd probably hear you better without all these bandages,' Bart said impatiently, raising his muffled hands towards his face.

'All in good time. Having any trouble breathing?'

'No, except for the bandages again.'

'Fine. You see, I changed the shape of your ears and nostrils; it might have affected your breathing and hearing, but it didn't. Now listen, Bart, I'm going to take the bandages off your hands first. Sit down.'

Bart sat across the table from him, obediently extending his hands. Raynor Three said, 'Shut your eyes.'

'I want to see –'

'Do as you're told. Shut your eyes.'

'Oh, all right,' Bart grumbled, shut his eyes and felt Raynor Three's long fingers, smooth and skilful, working at the bandages. He felt air on the backs of his fingers.

'Move each finger as I touch it.'

Bart felt light touches on each finger, first in turn, then irregularly moving from finger to finger. Raynor drew a breath of satisfaction and said, 'Good. All right, now, take a deep breath –'

'What's that got to do with –'

'Take a deep breath,' repeated Raynor inflexibly, 'and then open your eyes.'

Impatiently Bart breathed deep, and his lids flashed open. His breath went out in a harsh, jolting gasp. In spite of being prepared by photographs and in other ways for the disguise, it was still a shock to unseat reason. His hands lay on the table before him, but – *they were not his hands!*

The smooth, long, narrow fingers were pearl-grey, tipped with whitish-pink claws that curved smoothly over the finger-ends. Nervously, running his tongue over his lips, Bart moved one finger and the long claw flicked out like a cat's; retracted. He gasped again; swallowed.

'Golly!' He saw that the grey-clawed hands were shaking. He felt strangely wobbly.

'A beautiful job, if I do say so,' Raynor said. 'Be careful not to scratch yourself with them, now. And practise picking up small things. And writing in Lhari script.'

Bart swallowed. 'How did you make the claws?'

'Quite simple, really.' Raynor beamed. 'I injected protein compounds into the nail matrix, which speeded up the growth terrifically, and then, as they grew, shaped them. Joining on those tiny muscles for the retracting mechanism was the tricky part, though. Fortunately, human and Lhari hands are similar enough, otherwise – I'd have hated to have to take off a finger or try to graft one.'

Bart was moving his hands experimentally. Once over the shock, they felt quite normal. The claws didn't get in his way half as much as he'd expected when he picked up a pen that lay beside him and, with the blunt tip, made a few of the strange-looking dots and wedges that were the Lhari alphabet.

'Practise writing this,' said Raynor Three, and laid a plastic-encased folder down beside him. It was a set of ship's papers printed in Lhari; Bart read it through, seeing that it was made out to the equivalent of Astrogator First Class Bartol.

'That's your name now; the name your father would have used. Memorise it, get used to the sound of it, practise writing it. Don't worry too much about the rating; it's an elementary one, what we'd call Apprentice rating, and I have a training tape for you anyhow. My brother got hold of it, don't ask me how – and don't ask him! Probably by a little forgery that amounted to theft.'

'When am I going to see my face?' Bart asked.

'When I think you're ready for the shock,' Raynor said bluntly. 'It almost threw you when I showed you your hands.'

He made Bart walk around some more before he slowly unwound the bandages; then turned and picked up a mirror at the bottom of his Medic's case, turning it right side up. 'Here. But take it easy.'

But when Bart looked in the mirror he felt no unexpected shock, only an overwhelming curiosity and strangeness, and an unnerving revulsion. The face of a Lhari looked out at him from the mirror.

His hair was bleached-white and fluffy, almost feathery to the touch. His skin was greyish-rose, and his eyelids had been altered just enough in shape that his eyes looked long, narrow and slanted. His nostrils were mere slits in a sharp, delicate nose, and he felt very strange as he moved his tongue over lips that felt oddly thin.

'Lucky we didn't have to change your teeth very much,' Raynor Three told him. 'I did as little as I thought I could get away with – capped the front ones, that's all. So if you get a toothache, you're out of luck – you won't dare go to a Lhari dentist. I could have done more, but it would have made you look too freakish when we changed you back to human again – if you live through it,' he added rather grimly.

Bart said, 'I hadn't thought much about that. But – I *can* be changed back again?'

And if Raynor Three is going to forget me, who will do it – ? The cold knot of fear, never wholly absent, clawed at him again. Watching his face, Raynor Three said gently, 'It's a big network, Bart. I'm not telling you too much, for your own safety. But after you get to Antares, they'll contact you and tell you what you need to know. They're not Mentorians; you can talk with them freely.

71

They don't even have much contact with the Lhari. They'll make the arrangements.'

He added, lifting Bart's oddly clawed hands, 'I warned you, remember, the change isn't completely – reversible. Your hands will always look a bit – strange; the fingers had to be lengthened, for instance. But I wanted to make you as safe as possible among the Lhari. As it is, I think you'll pass everything but an X-ray. Just be careful not to break any bones.'

He gave Bart a package. 'This is the Lhari training tape. Listen to it as often as you possibly can, then destroy it *completely* – better burn it and scatter the ash – before you leave here. You can stay here a week; there's plenty of food. The *Swiftwing* is due in port three days from now, and they stay here a week. Give our people 48 hours – spend the time exercising, practise writing, and so forth – after they dock; then go in to town and sign in on the *Swiftwing*. I don't know how we'll manage it, but I'll guarantee there'll be a vacancy for one Astrogator First Class on that ship. Well –' he rose, 'I'm going back to town tonight, and erase this memory.' He stopped, looking intently at Bart.

'So, if you see me, Bart – stay away from me and don't speak. Because I won't know you from any odd Lhari – and I'll be just another Mentorian. Understand? From here on out – you're on your own – Bartol.'

'I don't know what to say,' Bart faltered, 'or how to thank you –'

'Don't try,' Raynor Three said bleakly. 'I liked your father. And I believe in what he was doing, or I'd never take so many risks. Well –' he held out his hand. 'This is the rough part, son. I'm in a strange position.' His face moved strangely. 'I'm part of this network they have between the stars – but I don't know what I've done before, and I'll never know how it comes out, or even what part I had in it. It's odd to stand here and look at you, and realise I won't even remember you.' The strange, gold-glinted eyes blinked rapidly. 'Goodbye, Bart. And – good luck.'

Bart took his hand, deeply moved, with the strange sense that this was another death, a worse one than Briscoe's. He felt dreadfully alone. He tried to speak and couldn't.

'Well –' Raynor's mouth tilted up in a wry grin, 'I could stand here and give you good advice all day. Ouch! Careful with those claws, boy! No wonder the Lhari don't shake hands!'

He turned abruptly and went out of the door and out of the gate and out of Bart's life, while Bart stood at the dome-window, looking down at his fantastic clawed hands, feeling alone as he had never felt alone before; not even when Raynor told him of his father's death.

Just another cog in a vast net between the stars – not Bart Steele, Vegan, any more. Resolutely, he picked up the blunt-tipped stylus and began to practise writing his Lhari signature.

He had to wait six days, and they felt like six eternities. He played the training tape over and over again, becoming familiar with the vocabulary of a Lhari Astrogator First Class and with the objects to which they referred. With his Space Academy background, it wasn't nearly as difficult as he'd feared. He read and re-read the set of papers that identified him as Astrogator First Class Bartol. Forged, he supposed. Or was there, somewhere, a real Lhari named Bartol? According to these papers, he had worked only on the Polaris run – a distant part of the galaxy; the chances of anyone on the *Swiftwing's* crew ever having been anywhere near that division were vanishingly small. That kind of one-in-a-million chance they couldn't guard against.

The last morning he slept uneasily late, dreaming of Briscoe, of his father, of Raynor Three. He finished his

last meal as a human, spent part of the day removing all
traces of his presence from Raynor's home, put his
clothes into the disposal, burnt the training tape, and
finally got into the silky, silvery tights and cloak that
Raynor had provided. He could use his hands now as if
they belonged to him – he even found the claws handy
and useful. He could write his signature and copy out
instructions from the training tape in Lhari script
without an instant's hesitation. He remembered having
read somewhere that the Lhari alphabet derived from a
primitive way of writing in soft wax or mud with their
claw-tips directly, in small dots and wedges like ancient
human cuneiform.

Towards dusk, a young Lhari slipped unobserved out
of Raynor's country house and hiked unnoticed to the
edges of a small city nearby, where he mingled with the
crowd and hired a skycab from an unobservant human
driver to take him to the spaceport city. The skycab
driver was startled, but not, Bart judged, unusually so,
to pick up a Lhari passenger.

'Been doing a little sightseeing on our planet, hey?'

'That's right,' Bart said in Universal, not trying to
fake his idea of the Lhari accent. Raynor had told him
that only a few of the Lhari had the characteristic
sibilant 'r' and 's' and warned him against trying to
imitate it. *Just speak naturally; there are dialects of Lhari, just
as there are dialects of the different human languages, and they
all sound different in Universal anyhow.* 'Just looking around
some.'

The skycab driver frowned and looked down at his
controls, and Bart felt curiously snubbed. Then he
remembered. He, himself, had little to say to the Lhari
when they spoke to him.

*He was an alien, a monster. He couldn't expect to be treated
like a human being any more.*

When the skycab let him off before the spaceport, it

74

felt strange to see how the crowds edged away from him as he made a way through them. He caught a glimpse of himself in one of the mirror-ramps, a tall thin form in a metallic cloak, head crested with feathery white, and felt overwhelmingly homesick for his own familiar face.

He was beginning to feel hungry, and realised that he could not go into an ordinary restaurant without attracting attention; it was something the Lhari did very rarely – he supposed, resentfully, that they were 'slumming' or something, when they did. There were refreshment stands all over the spaceport, and he briefly considered getting a snack at one of these.

No, that was just putting it off. The time had to come when he must face his fear and test his disguise among the Lhari themselves. It might as well be now. Reviewing his knowledge of the construction of spaceports, he remembered that one side was the terminal, where humans and visitors and passengers were freely admitted; the other side, for Lhari and their Mentorian employees only, contained – along with business offices of many sorts – a sort of arcade with amusement centres, shops and restaurants catering to the personnel of the Lhari ships. With nine or ten ships docking every day, Raynor had assured him that a strange Lhari face would be lost in the crowds very easily.

He went to one of the doors marked *danger, Lhari Lights beyond*, and passed through the glaring corridor of offices and storage warehouses, finally coming out into a sort of wide mall. The lights were fierce, but he could endure them without trouble now, though his head ached faintly. Raynor, testing his light tolerance, had assured him that he could endure anything the Lhari could without permanent damage to his optic nerves, though he would have headaches until he got used to them.

There were small shops and what looked like bars, and a glass-fronted place with a sign lettered largely, in black letters, a Lhari phrase meaning roughly HOME AWAY FROM HOME: MEALS SERVED, SPACE-MEN WELCOME, REASONABLE.

He stood hesitating before the restaurant, touched with last-minute panic.

Behind him, a voice said in the Lhari language, 'Tell me, does that sign really mean what it says? Or is this one of those traps for separating the unwary spaceman from his hard-earned credits? How's the food?'

Bart carefully took hold of himself. Now was the real test.

'I don't know; I've never eaten here,' he said carefully, 'I was just wondering that myself. I suppose it's like most of these places: good if you don't mind paying for what you get.' He turned as he spoke, and found himself face to face with a young Lhari in the unadorned cloak, like Bart himself, of a spaceman without official rank. He knew the Lhari was young because his crest was still white, his face unlined as Bart's own.

The young Lhari extended his claws in the closed-fist, hidden-claw gesture of Lhari greeting and said, 'Shall we take a chance? Ringg son of Rahan greets you.'

'Bartol son of Berihin,' Bart said, returning the closed-fist gesture, speaking his alias for the first time.

The young Lhari pushed the door, his thin lips drawing back in a smile, as he remarked, 'New here? I don't remember seeing you in the port, but there are so many –'

'I've been working through this end of the Galaxy,' Bart said. This was the agreed-on story. 'But I've mostly signed on the Polaris run.'

'Way off there?' The Lhari sounded startled and impressed. 'You really get around, don't you? Shall we sit here?'

76

They sat on triangular chairs at a three-cornered table. Bart noticed that one chair was blue, the other two an odd orange colour, but he knew the Lhari could not see colours; the texture of the two was identical. He waited for Ringg son of Rahan to order, and ordered what he did; when it came, it was a sort of egg-and-fish casserole which Bart found extremely tasty, and he found himself digging into it with pleasure. Allowing for the claws, Lhari table manners were not appreciably different from human – *and remember, their customs vary as much as ours do. If you do something differently, they'll just think you come from a different part of some planet or other!*

Feeling, after a short time, that his new acquaintance was waiting for him to make some remark, Bart asked, 'Have you been at this port for long?'

'A day or so. I'm off the *Swiftwing*.'

Bart decided swiftly to try his luck. He said, 'I was told there's a vacancy on the *Swiftwing*.'

Ringg raised his head and looked at him with some curiosity. 'There is,' he said, 'though I'd like to know how you found it out! Captain Vorongil said that anyone who talked about it would be sent to Kleeto for three cycles! What happened to you, though? Miss your ship?'

'No, I've just been laying off – travelling, sightseeing a little, doing odd jobs here and there, bumming around,' Bart said. Raynor Three had told him that a good many of the younger Lhari did this, evidently motivated by sheer curiosity about human ways and customs, though usually on the friendlier planets near the original Mentorian planet of contact. 'But I'm tired of it and I want to sign on and ship out again.'

The young Lhari looked worried.

'It's this way,' Ringg said. 'If Captain Vorongil knows that there's been talk in the port about Klanerol jumping ship, or whatever happened to him, he'll make our lives a burden to us. Just the same, it's true, we *are* short one man, and it won't be pleasant. It's all right for these short hops, but this is the long run we're making out to Antares and then home. If all the men have to run extra shifts that's no fun for anybody. If we could pick up a man here, you – what's your name, Bartol?'

Bart nodded.

'Well, Bartol, listen here. Don't tell Vorongil that you heard about it in port, or we'll have to face his temper!'

Bart was beginning to relax a little. Ringg apparently accepted him without scrutiny and didn't think him strange. At this close range Ringg did not seem a monster but just a young fellow like himself, hearty, good-natured – in fact, Bart found himself thinking that Ringg was not unlike Tom! He chased the thought away as soon as it sneaked into his brain – one of those *things*, like Tom? Then, he thought grimly, *I'm one of those things*, I've got to get along with them somehow. He said, rather irritably, 'So then, how do I account for asking your Captain for the place?'

Ringg cocked his fluffy crest to one side and thought for a minute. 'I know,' he said. '*I* told you. I'll say you're an old friend of mine, and when I saw you here, I suggested you sign out with us. You don't know what Vorongil's like when he gets mad! If you walk in from a human world and tell him the port's full of gossip about someone deserting from his ship, he won't be fit to live with. Who *did* tell you, anyhow?'

This was the first real hurdle, and Bart thought about it desperately. But before he could answer, Ringg said with blistering scorn, 'I suppose some of the men gossiped in a bar and one of those fool Mentorians picked it up.'

'Well,' said Bart, 'talk gets around that way sometimes.'

Ringg shrugged. 'What Vorongil doesn't know, he won't shout about.' He shoved back the triangular chair. 'Got your papers? What's your rating?'

'Astrogator First Class.'

'Klanerol was Second, but you can't have everything, I suppose,' Ringg said, and led the way through the arcades, out across a guarded sector, passing half a dozen of the huge ships lying in their pits. Finally, at the edge of one of the pits, Ringg stopped and pointed.

'This is the old hulk. Nothing new and fancy here.'

Bart had travelled only on the Lhari passenger ships, which were new and fresh and sleek. This one was enormous, ovoid like the egg of some space monster, the sides dented and discoloured from unimaginable strains, thin films of chemical colouring lying over the glassy metallic hull. Great black letters gave the Lhari word that meant *Swiftwing*. Bart knew he was staring, and Ringg poked him.

'Watch your feet on the catwalk, Bartol.'

Below, men and Lhari, supervised by Mentorians, were working on service crews. Bart tore his eyes away and followed Ringg. This was real, it was happening. He was signing out for his first interstellar cruise on one of the Lhari ships. Not a Mentorian assistant, half-trusted, half-tolerated – but one of the crew themselves. *If I'm lucky*, he reminded himself grimly.

There was a Lhari, in the black-banded officer's cloak, at the doorway. He glanced at Ringg's papers.

'Friend of mine,' Ringg said, and Bart proffered his folder. The Lhari gave it a casual glance, handed it back.

'Old man on board?' Ringg asked.

'Where else?' The officer laughed. 'You don't think *he'd* relax with cargo not loaded, do you?'

They seemed casual and normal, and Bart's confidence was growing. They had accepted him as one of themselves. His Lhari would serve, and so far no slang phrase or small habit of the culture had tripped him up.

But the great ordeal still lay before him – an interview with the Lhari captain. And the idea had Bart sick, shaking, sweating scared. His feet fumbled on the ramps within the ship.

Why did I ever get into this? By now, I'd have been safe home on Vega!

Well, you had your chance.

The corridors and decks seemed larger, wider, more spacious, but shabbier than on the clean, bright commercial passenger decks Bart had seen. Men, dark-lensed, were rolling bales of cargo along on wheeled dollies. The corridors seemed endless. More to hear the sound of his own voice, and reassure himself of his ability to speak and be understood, than because he cared, he asked Ringg, 'What's your rating?'

'Well, according to the logbooks, I'm an Expert Class Two, Metals-Fatigue,' said Ringg. 'That sounds very technical and interesting. But what it means is just that I go all over the ship inch by inch, and when I finish, start all over again at the other end. Most of what I do is just boss around the maintenance crews and snarl at them about spots of rust on the paint!'

They got into a small round elevator and Ringg punched buttons; it began to rise, slowly and creakily, towards the top. 'This, for instance,' Ringg said. 'I've been yelling for a new cable for six months.' He turned. 'Take it easy, Bartol, don't let Vorongil scare you. He likes to hear the sound of his own voice, but we'd all walk out the lock without spacesuits for him!'

The elevator slid to a stop. The sign in Lhari letters said *Level of Administration* – Officers Deck. Ringg pushed at a door and said, 'Captain Vorongil?'

'I thought you were on leave,' said a Lhari voice, deeper and slower than most. 'What are you doing, back here more than ten milliseconds before strap-in checks?'

Ringg stepped back for Bart to go inside. The small

cabin, with an elliptical bunk slung from the ceiling and a triangular table, was dwarfed by a tall, thin Lhari, in a cloak with four of the black bands that seemed to denote rank among them. He had a deeply-lined face with a thousand small wrinkles around the long slant-eyes, and the fluffy white of his crest was broken short at the scalp, and yellowed with age. Bart had the sudden, prickly feeling that he had seen this old Lhari before. He forced himself to be calm; that was light-years away, and he was not himself any more.

'Come in, young fellow,' the old Lhari said. I suppose Rahan's-son here has been telling you what a tyrant I am.' He sounded amused. 'What do you want, white-heads?' (Bart supposed that was the Lhari equivalent of 'kids' or 'youngsters'.) Ringg looked exasperated.

Bart reached into the capacious fold of his cloak for his papers, thrust out his closed-fist in greeting. His voice sounded shrill, even to himself. 'Bartol son of Berihin greets you, *rieko mori*.' (Honourable Bald One; the Lhari equivalent of *sir*.) 'Ringg told me there is a – a vacancy among the Astrogators, sir, and I want to sign out.'

Unmistakeably, Vorongil's snort was laughter. 'So you have been talking, Ringg! Your tongue is like a bell-rope!'

'Which makes no noise without someone to ring it,' Ringg retorted. 'Better that I tell him, than that you have to hunt the planet over for someone stationed here – or ship on the big run with one man short in the drives chamber! That Mentorian girl can't do it all herself!'

'Well, well, you're right,' Vorongil snorted. He growled at Bart, 'On our last stop, one of our men vanished. Jumped ship! Never said a word or signed out, just walked off. We can't hunt around on strange worlds –' but the creases around the eyes deepened. 'If I thought he'd just gone off on the drift, sightseeing, I would be sore, but I wish he'd told me. I'm not such an old shouter as all that!' He scowled. 'As it is, I keep wondering if he's been hurt, killed, kidnapped.'

Ringg said, 'Who'd dare? It would be reported. We checked the hospitals, remember.'

Bart knew suddenly, with a shower of cold chills, that Klanerol had not simply gone 'on the drift' as young Lhari were supposed to do sometimes. He was sure that no Lhari port would ever see Klanerol again. *Another death!*

This was for keeps, remember.

'Bartol,' mused Vorongil, looking at Bartol's forged papers. 'I see you're an expert at Second Galaxy mathematics. Served on the Polaris run. Hm. You *are* off your orbit, aren't you? Never been out that way myself. I can't check your maths knowledge because I don't know much myself; that's what we get for putting everything in the hands of technical people. All right, I'll take you on. You can do system computation programming? Good.' He hauled out a sheet of thin wax and his claws made rapid imprints in the surface; Bart watched, fascinated. He passed it to Bart; pointed. Bart hesitated, not sure, and Vorongil said impatiently, 'It's the standard one – no hidden clauses. Put your mark on it, white-head.'

Bart realised it was something like a fingerprint they wanted. *You'll pass anything but X-rays.* He pressed the tip of one claw into the wax. Vorongil nodded and shoved it on a shelf without looking at it.

'So much for that,' said Ringg, laughing, as they came out. 'The Bald One was in a good temper for once. I'm going back to the port and celebrate, not that this dim planet is very festive. You?'

'I – I think I'll stay aboard.'

'Well, if you change your mind, I'll be down there somewhere,' Ringg said. 'See you later, shipmate.' He raised his closed fist in farewell, and went.

Bart stood in the corridor, not quite sure where to go next, but he meant to do some exploring, now that he was signed on and had a right to be there. He felt astounded and strange. *He belonged here!* This was where he would live and work, this was where he would find the secret of the stars!

This was where he would spy. . . .

A Lhari, as short and fat as a Lhari could possibly be and still be a Lhari, came or rather waddled out of the Captain's office. He saw Bartol and called, 'Are you the new First-Class? I'm Rugel, co-ordinator.'

Rugel had a huge cleft purplish scar across his lip, so dark that Bart was sure it must be visible even to Lhari eyes as darkness if not as colour, and his cloak had two bands. He was completely bald, older even than Vorongil, and he puffed when he walked. 'Vorongil asked me to show you around, white-head. You'll have Klanerol's quarters – he said you're a friend of Ringg's already, so there's no sense shifting another man, and you two young fellows ought to get along pretty well. Come on down and see the chart rooms – or do you want to leave your kit in your cabin first?'

'I don't have much,' Bart said.

Rugel's seamed lip widened. 'That's the way, travel light when you're on the drift,' he confirmed. 'Been off long? If you're short of credit, you know, you can get an advance in port: the Second Officer's pretty decent.'

Bart shook his head. 'I've enough, thanks.' Raynor had changed his money for Lhari credits.

Rugel took him down to the drive rooms, and here for a moment, in wonder and awe, Bart almost forgot his disguise. The old Lhari led him to the huge computer which filled one wall of the room, and Bart was smitten with the universality of mathematics. Here was something he *knew* he could handle.

He could do this programming, easily enough. But as

he stood before the banks of complex, yet beautifully familiar levers, the sheer exquisite complexity of it overcame him. To compute the movements of thousands of stars, all moving at different speeds in different directions in the vast swirling directionless chaos of the Universe – and yet to be sure that every separate movement would come out to within a quarter of a mile! It was something that no finite brain – man or Lhari – could ever accomplish; yet their limited brains had built these computers that *could* do it!

Rugel watched him, laughing softly. 'Well, you'll have enough time down here. I like to have youngsters who are still in the middle of a love affair with their work. Come along, and I'll show you where your cabin is.'

Rugel took him to a cabin amidships and left him there. It was small and cramped, but tidy and comfortable, with two of the elliptical bunks slung at opposite ends, a small oval table between them, shelves along one side of the wall with sliding panels to keep their contents from falling out during the free-fall of acceleration surges, and drawers under the table, filled with assortments of pamphlets and manuals and maps. Swiftly, furtively, ashamed of himself yet driven by necessity, Bart searched Ringg's belongings, wanting to get some idea of what possessions it would be considered eccentric for him not to own. He looked around the shower and toilet facilities with extra care – this was something he *couldn't* slip up on and be considered even halfway normal Lhari. He was afraid Ringg would come in, and see him looking with attentive curiosity at something as ordinary, to a Lhari, as a cake of soap (the can of powdery detergent which the Lhari used instead of caked tablets of soap).

But after a time, alone there, he grew nervous. He decided to go down into the port again, and look around in the Lhari shops. You can learn a lot about people from what they buy. He was not afraid of failing to be able to do his work, or of slipping up in speech. What he feared was something subtler; that the small items of everyday living, something as simple as a nail file, would trip him up and betray him. Raynor, familiar with the Lhari through their medicine, had told him as much as he could. But he couldn't think of everything.

He found his way past the Recreation Room – filled with comfortable seats and tables in what looked to Bart like an eye-hurting jumble of colours, which of course the Lhari did not see – and visionscreens and what appeared to be simple pinball machines and mechanical games of skill. There were also stacks of tape-reels and headsets for listening, not at all unlike their human equivalents. Bart felt fascinated, and wanted to explore, but he could do that at leisure.

Somehow, he took the wrong turn out of the recreation room; he went through what should have been the door to the elevator to the lower part of the ship, and instead the dimming of the lights told him he was in a sector used by humans also. The sudden darkness made him stumble, thrust out his hands to keep himself from falling, and someone cried out.

'Ouch!' It was an unmistakably human voice.

'I'm sorry,' Bart said in Universal, without thinking. Immediately he realised it had been a mis-step, but it was too late to remedy now.

'I admit the lights are dim,' said the voice, tartly, 'but you might be prepared for that now, it seems.'

Bart blinked and found himself looking down at a girl.

She was small and slender in her cloak of metallic blue, sweeping out like wings around her thin arms; the hood framed a small kitten-like face, and short curls of red hair. She was a Mentorian, and she was human, and Bart let his eyes rest with comfort on her face; she, on the other hand, was looking at him with anxiety and uneasy distrust. *That's right, I'm a Lhari* – a nonhuman freak!

He said, still in Universal – it was good to hear a human tongue – 'I seem to have missed my way.'

'Oh, are you new on board, sir? What are you looking for? The Medical quarters are through here.'

'No, I'm looking for the lift down to the crew exits.'

'Through here,' she said, opening the door through which he had come, and shading her large, lovely, dark-lashed eyes with a slim hand. 'You took the wrong turn, sir. But I thought all ships were laid out the same way.'

He said, shifting to Lhari, 'I've only – worked on passenger ships.'

'Oh, I see; I believe they are a little different in layout,' said the girl in good Lhari. 'Well, that is your way, sir.'

He felt as if he had been snubbed and dismissed. 'What is your name?'

She straightened as if about to salute and said stiffly, 'Meta of the house of Marnay Two, sir.'

Bart suddenly realised that he was doing an incredible thing for a Lhari; standing and talking with one of the despised inferior race. With a wistful glance at the pretty girl, he said 'Thank you,' and went off in the direction she had pointed. He felt horribly lonely. He had lost the impulse to go out into the port again; he went back to the cabin, got into the elliptical bunk – it was very comfortable – and, expecting to lie awake for hours fretting, fell asleep so fast he did not even hear Ringg come in.

Chapter Seven

He saw the Mentorian girl again next day when they checked-in aboard before blast-off.

That morning, he and Ringg had gone together down to the port, and he had bought a few stray items of clothing, Lhari-style toilet articles – an oddly human-looking comb and electrical toothbrush, a manicure kit that reminded him of horse-shoeing equipment – various small odds and ends, and, unable to resist the temptation, bought a few books in Lhari, telling himself they would increase his comprehension of the alien customs.

The girl was seated at a small desk, triangular like so much of the Lhari furniture, checking a register as they came out of the decontamination chamber, making sure they downed their green solution of micro-organisms. Ringg made a wry face and the girl smiled as if to herself, then turned bland eyes up to Bartol.

'Your papers, please?' She looked at the name, marked the register. Bart noted she was using a red pencil. 'Bartol,' she said aloud. 'Is that how you pronounce it, sir?' Bart nodded and she made small markings in a sort of shorthand with the red pencil. She made other marks with a black one; he supposed the red one was her own private register, unreadable by the Lhari.

Ringg glanced over her shoulder and chuckled. 'I'm

in luck,' he said. 'You drew drive-room watch for Acceleration One, Bartol.'

The girl, Meta, said expressionlessly, 'That is quite right, Ringg. You are on duty below, and Bartol in the drive room for Acceleration One. Next, please.' She handed a cup of the greenish stuff to the Lhari behind them, a tall thin white-crested fellow in a cloak with two bands. 'Drive room watch for Acceleration One, sir. Strap-in check in seventeen minutes.'

He supposed she was a Medical Assistant of some sort. He found himself, as he went down to the drive-room, wishing that she were a mathematician, on duty in the drive and astrogation rooms, as his mother had been. It would have been pleasant to watch her.

Old Rugel was on duty in the drive room; he motioned Bart to a reclining couch before the big computer that was his station. He watched Bart strap himself in, reminding him, 'Be sure you check all your dials on zero, Bartol,' and Bart felt a last-minute, split-second surge of panic:

This was his first cruise! This was his first assignment! Yet his rating called him an experienced man on the faraway Polaris run! He'd had the Lhari training tape, which was supposed to condition his responses – but would it be adequate? He tried to clench his fists, drove a claw into his palm, winced, and commanded himself to stay calm and remember where he was and what he was doing.

It calmed him, a little, to make the routine check of the dials and studs of the computers before him. Back at the Space Academy, he had worked the Astrogation post in dozens of simulated takeoffs, rated 'Excellent' and 'Superior', on testing cruises in the academy training ship. The Lhari training tape would take care of the differences between them. A takeoff from a planet was a takeoff from a planet; Earth, Vega or Procyon

Alpha. He could handle this.

'Strap-in check,' said a Lhari with a yellowed crest and a rasping voice. 'New man, eh?' He bent and gave Bart's straps perfunctory tugs at shoulders, waist, tightened a buckle. He made a brief closed-fist gesture of greeting. 'Karol son of Garan.'

Bart spoke his own alias, quite naturally by now.

Bells rang in the ship, and Bart felt the odd, tonic little touch of fear. *This is it.* Far down in the ship, a curious low humming sound vibrated.

Vorongil strode through the door, his tall banded cloak sweeping behind him, and took the empty central couch. He submitted politely to the checking officer's ministrations, waved him away.

'Catalyst,' Vorongil said roughly in Lhari.

'Ready from fuelling room, sir,' an officer reported.

'Position.'

Bart heard himself reading off a string of figures in Lhari, his voice perfectly calm.

'Communication.'

'Clear channels from Pylon Dispatch, sir.' It was old Rugel's voice.

'Well,' Vorongil said, slowly and almost reflectively. 'Let's take her up, then.'

He touched some controls. The humming grew. Then a swift crushing weight mashed Bart against his couch.

'Position!' Vorongil's voice sounded harsh, and Bart fought the crushing weight of it. Even his eyeballs ached as he struggled to turn the tiny eye muscles from dial to dial, and his voice was a dim croak.

'Fourteen seven sidereal twelve point one one four nine....'

'Hold it to point one one four six.'

'Point one one four six,' Bart said, and his claws stabbed at the dials. Suddenly, in spite of the cold weight on his chest, the pain, the struggle, he felt as if he were floating. He managed a long, luxurious breath. He *could* handle it. He knew what he was doing.

He was an Astrogator. . . .

Later, when Acceleration One had reached its apex and the artificial gravity made the ship a place of comfort again, he went down to the dining hall with Ringg and met the crew of the *Swiftwing*. There were twelve officers and twelve crewmen of various ratings like himself and Ringg, but there seemed to be little social division between them. None of them gave him a second look, and all of them were so busy talking about their leave in port that they had no questions for a greenhorn Astrogator who had signed on in place of one gone 'on the drift.' After the meal, in the Recreation Room, Ringg challenged him to a game with one of the pinball-type machines. It seemed fairly simple to Bart; he tried it, rather dubiously, and to his surprise, won.

Ringg touched a lever at the side of the room; with a tiny whishing sound, shutters opened, the light of Procyon Alpha flooded them, and he looked out through a vast, quartzite window into clear bottomless space.

'Don't do that,' said one of the young officers, in a high, complaining voice, 'it makes the floor go out from under me.'

'Fine thing – shipping out for a spaceman when you're afraid of heights,' Ringg said genially. The two young Lhari cuffed and jostled one another playfully, like a pair of kittens pretending to fight, claws retracted; arguing over the lever, pretending to struggle for it. Bart saw them only in a daze. The ringed planets of Procyon, Alpha, Beta and Gamma hung at full, their green and blue and golden rings tilted gently, receding into the distance. Past them the stars burned, flaming through the shimmers of cosmic dust. The colours, the never-ending colours of space! He sought, grasping at reality, for the deep flame of Antares where they were bound.

It was like a *red* eye. . . .

In shock, he realised that while he was thinking in Lhari, he had had to shift back to Universal for the name of the colour. He stood here, in a room full of strange creatures, monsters, and he was one of the monsters; staring at a sight which only he could behold!

'Which one of the planets was it we stopped on?' Karol asked. 'I can't tell them apart from this distance. Bartol, can you?'

The blue one, he thought; Beta was golden, Gamma green; but he choked the words back and pointed, saying, 'The big one there, with the rings almost edge-on. I think they call it *Alpha*.'

'It's their planet,' Karol said, 'I guess they can call it anything they want to. How about another game, Bartol?'

Resolutely, Bartol turned his back on the bewitching colours and bent over the pinball machine.

The first week in space was a nightmare of strain. He welcomed the hours spent in the drive room on watch because only there was he sure of himself. Before the big computer he could make no mistakes. But everywhere else in the ship he was perpetually scared, perpetually on tiptoe, perpetually afraid of making some small and stupid mistake. Once he actually called Aldebaran a red star, but Rugel either did not hear the slip or thought he was repeating what one of the Mentorians – there were two in the drive room, a quiet elderly man and a middle-aged woman – had said.

The absence of colour from speech and life was the hardest thing to get used to. Every star listed in his computer handbook was listed by frequency waves, and could be checked against a light meter for a specific frequency reading, and it nearly drove Bart mad to go carefully through the ritual when the Mentorians were off duty and could not call off the colour and the equivalent frequency. Yet he did not dare to skip a single step, or someone might have guessed that he could actually *see* the colour difference between a yellow and a green star before reading the difference between their two wavelengths on the light meter.

And the Academy ships had had the traditional danger signals of flashing red lights. Unaccustomed to a colourless panel, Bart was stretched taut continually, waiting for the small buzzers and ticks that warned of dials too far to the left or right, machinery out of order somewhere, leads and wires in need of servicing. On one off-watch, he observed Ringg going through the ship with his metals-fatigue testing equipment – a bewildering small array of boxes, meters, gauges, rods and earphones – and felt dizzy at the unfathomable sounds.

At first it was all a bedlam to him; he felt stretched to capacity every waking moment, perpetually a-tiptoe for danger, for some slip, watching his tongue, his hands, his ears with fanatic care. He burdened his aching memory with a million details, lay awake nights mentally going over the combinations of the small signals that meant one thing or another. He felt as if his mind would crack under the strain. Alpha faded to a dim bluish shimmer, Beta was eclipsed, Gamma was gone, Procyon dimmed to a falling spark; and suddenly, Bart's memory accustomed itself to the load, the new habits were firmly in place, and he found himself eating, sleeping and working in a settled routine.

He belonged to the *Swiftwing*, now.

Procyon was almost lost in the viewport when a sort of upswept tempo began to run through the ship, an undercurrent of increased activity. Cargo was checked, inventoried and strapped in. Ringg was given four extra men to help him, made an extra tour of the ship, and came back buzzing like a frantic cricket. Bart's computers told him they were forging towards the sidereal location assigned for the first of the warpdrive shifts, which would take them some fifteen light-years towards Aldebaran.

On the final watch before the warpdrive shift, the Medical officer came around and relieved the Mentorians from duty. Bart watched them go, with a curious crawling apprehension. Even the Mentorians, trusted by the Lhari – even these were put into coldsleep! Fear grabbed his insides. *No human had ever survived the shift into warpdrive*, the Lhari said. Briscoe, his father, Raynor Three – they thought they had proved that the Lhari lied. If they were right, if it was a Lhari trick to reinforce their stranglehold on the human worlds and keep the warpdrive for themselves, then Bart had nothing to fear. But he was afraid.

He thought of the girl Meta, whom he had not seen since the first day of Acceleration One. The Mentorians had their own recreation quarters and did not mingle with the Lhari. Bart thought of his own mother, like this on a Lhari ship, alone. Why did they do it?

What had Raynor said? *Because I belong in space, because I'm never happy anywhere else.* Bart looked out of the viewport, watching the swirl and burn of the colours there. They seemed somehow to symbolise the thing he could never put into words: why he was doing this. *So that everyone can have this. Not just the Lhari.*

It kept his fear away.

Old Rugel watched the Mentorians go, scowling. 'I wish Medic would hurry up and find some way to keep them alive through warpshift,' he said. 'My Mentorian assistant could watch that frequency-shift as we got near the bottom of the arc, and I'll bet he could *see* it. They can see changes in intensity faster than I can work them out on the photometer!'

Bart felt goose bumps breaking out on his skin. Rugel

spoke, even though he thought only Lhari were present, as if the death of humans, Mentorians, in warpdrive was a fact! Didn't the Lhari themselves *know* it was a farce? *Or was he tricked....*

Vorongil himself took the controls for the surge of Acceleration Two – which would take them up past the L-point, the point where the unknown catalyst would begin to generate the rays of the warpdrive. Bart, watching his instruments to exact position and time, saw the colours of each star shift strangely, moment by moment. The red stars seemed hard to see. The orange-yellow ones burned suddenly like flame; the green ones seemed golden, the blue ones almost green.... dimly he remembered the old story of a 'red shift' in the lights of approaching stars, but here he saw it pure, a sight that perhaps no human eyes had ever seen. A sight that *no* eyes had seen, human or otherwise, for the Lhari could not see it....

'Time,' he said briefly to Vorongil, 'Fifteen seconds –'

Rugel looked across at him from his couch, his eyes narrowed kindly. Bart felt that old, scarred Lhari could read his fear. Rugel said through a wheeze, 'No matter how old you get, Bartol, you're still scared when you make a warpshift. But relax, computers don't make mistakes.'

'Catalyst,' Vorongil snapped, 'Ready – *shift!*'

At first there was no change; then Bart realised that the stars, through the viewport, had altered abruptly in size and shade and colour. They were not sparks but strange streaks, like comets crossing and recrossing, tails that grew longer and longer, moment by moment. The dark night of space was filled with a crisscrossing blaze. They were moving faster than light, they saw the light left by the moving universe as each star hurled in its own invisible orbit, while they tore incredibly through it, faster than light itself....

Bart felt a curious tingling discomfort, deep in his flesh; almost an itching, a stinging in his very bones.

Lhari flesh is no different from ours. . . .

Space, seen through the viewport, was no longer space as he had come to know it, but a strange eerie limbo, the star-tracks lengthening, shifting colour until they filled the whole viewport with shimmering, grey, recrossing light. The unbelievable reaction of warpdrive thrust them through space, faster than the lights of the surrounding stars, faster than imagination could follow. . . .

The lights in the drive chamber began to dim . . . or was he blacking out? The stinging in his flesh was a clawed pain.

Briscoe lived through it . . .

They say.

The whirling star-tracks fogged, coiled, turned colourless worms of light, went into a single vast blur. Dimly Bart saw old Rugel slump forward, moaning softly; saw the old Lhari pillow his bald head on his veined arms. Then darkness took him; thinking it was death, Bart felt only numb, regretful failure. *I've failed, we'll always fail. The Lhari were right all along.*

But we tried! By God, we tried!

'Bartol?' A gentle hand, catclaws retracted, came down on his shoulder. Ringg bent over him. Good-natured rebuke was in his voice. 'Why didn't you tell us you got the bad reaction, and ask to sign out for this shift?' he demanded. 'Look, poor old Rugel's passed out again. He just won't admit he can't take it – but one idiot on a watch is enough! Some people just feel as if the bottom's dropped out of the ship, and that's all there is to it.'

Bart hauled his head upright, fighting a surge of stinging nausea. His bones itched inside and he was damnably uncomfortable, but he was alive. He made an

95

indistinct sound, then found that his mouth and tongue, though stiff, would obey him. 'I'm – fine.'

'You look it,' Ringg said in derision. 'Feel better? Think you can help me get Rugel to his cabin?'

Bart struggled to his feet, and found that when he was upright he felt better. 'Wow!' he muttered, then clamped his mouth shut. He was supposed to be an experienced man, a Lhari hardened to space. He said woozily, 'How long was I out?'

'The usual time,' Ringg said briskly, 'about three seconds – just while we hit peak warpdrive. Feels longer so they tell me, sometimes – time's funny, beyond light-speeds. The Medic says it's purely psychological. I'm not so sure. I *itch*, blast it!' He moved his shoulders in a squirming way, then bent over Rugel, who was moaning, half sensible. 'Catch hold of his feet, Bartol. Here – ease him out of his chair. No sense bothering the Medics this time. Think you can manage to help me carry him down to the deck?'

'Sure,' Bart said, finding his feet and his voice. He felt better as they moved along the hallway, the limp, muttering form of the old Lhari insensible in their arms. They reached the officer's deck, got Rugel into his cabin and into his bunk, hauled off his cloak and boots and covered him up with a blanket; Ringg stood shaking his head as they snapped out the light.

'And they say Captain Vorongil's so tough!'

Bart made a questioning noise.

'Why, just look,' said Ringg. 'He knows it would make poor old Rugel feel as if he wasn't good for much – to order him into his bunk and make him take dope like a Mentorian for every warpshift! So we have this to go through, at every jump!' He sounded cross and disgusted, but there was a rough, boyish gentleness as he hauled the blanket over the bald old Lhari. He looked up, almost shyly.

'You feeling better, Bartol? Want the Medic?'

'I'm fine,' Bart said again, and meant it. With the knowledge that even the Lhari suffered occasional discomfort and painful reactions to the warpdrive, his own feelings of nausea and prickling had seemed to diminish.

'Thanks for helping me with Old Baldy. We usually try to get him out before Vorongil officially takes notice. Of course, he sort of keeps his back turned,' Ringg said, and they laughed together as they turned back to the drive room. Bart found himself thinking, Ringg's a good kid, before he pulled himself up, in sudden shock.

He *had* lived through warpdrive! Then indeed, the Lhari had been lying all along; the vicious lie that maintained their stranglehold monopoly on star travel between systems! His brief accord with them vanished. He was their enemy again, the spy within their gates, the one who would live through it and bear back the word – not like Briscoe, to be hunted down and killed, but to bring the message, loud and clear, to everyone: *The Lhari lied! The stars can belong to us all!*

When he got back to the drive room, he saw through the viewport that the blur had vanished; the star-trails were clear, distinct, comet-trails again, their tails shortening by the moment; their colours clearing, growing more distinct. The Lhari in the drive room were evidently just waiting for the process to end; some were poised over their instruments, a few were standing near the quartzite viewport watching the curious panorama of star-trails, and four or five were squirming and scratching and grousing about what they called 'space fleas' – the characteristic itching reaction which seemed to be deep down inside their bones and seemed to be a not unusual reaction to faster-than-light speeds.

Bart checked his own computer panel, noted the time and position when they would snap back into normal space again, and went to stand by the viewport. The stars were reappearing, seeming to steady and blaze out in cloudy splendour through their veils of bright dust. They burned at him in great streamers of flame, and for a moment he forgot his mission again, lost in the bounty of fiery lights. He drew a deep, shaking gasp. It was worth it all, to see this! He turned and saw Ringg standing, silent, at his shoulder.

'Me, too,' Ringg said, almost in a whisper, 'only don't tell them I'm such a half-crested nestling, either. Just between you and me, I think every man on the ship feels that way a little. Only he won't admit it. Afraid of being laughed at, I guess.' His slanted grey eyes moved quickly to Bart and away again. 'Only – it's beautiful. I don't care what you say, it's beautiful.'

Two hours later, Bart checked his instrument panels and discovered that they were inside the Aldebaran system. This made the report official, and a Medic was dispatched to wake up the Mentorians. The stars were their own familiar colours again.

The *Swiftwing* moved on between the stars at incredible speeds. Aldebaran gave way to another star whose human name Bart did not know, and another; warpdrive shift followed warpdrive shift, system followed system, and Bart's memory amassed memorized coordinates aplenty, even though he knew they would not touch the important fuelling world until after they had reached Antares. On some of these planets, Men lived, and the Lhari spaceport rose alien and arrogant to the skies, and on each of these worlds men looked at the Lhari with resentful eyes, cursing this race who kept the stars for their own. And Bart moved among them, one of the Lhari, seeing the eyes of his own people fixed on him with hate, thinking with an almost comfortable self-pity:

I'm doing this for you. Some day, when I've given you the stars, you'll know....

Cargo followed cargo in the *Swiftwing*'s hold; loading and off-loading, landings on airless moons where all the work was done by robot machinery, on deserted worlds where men had never been. Bart grew – not bored, but accustomed to the incredible. For days at a time not a single word of human speech crossed even his mind.

The moment of blackout at the bottom of each warpshift persisted; Vorongil had given him the chance to report off duty, but since the momentary blackout did not impair his efficiency, Bart refused. Rugel told him that this was the moment of equilibrium, where the utter peak of that faster-than-light motion was reached.

'Perhaps a true limiting speed beyond which nothing will ever go,' Captain Vorongil said, touching the charts with a varnished claw. Rugel's scarred old mouth spread in a thin smile.

'Maybe there's no such thing as a limiting speed, Captain. Some day we'll reach true simultaneity – enter warp, and come out where we want to be, at the same time. Just a split second interval. That will be real matter-transmission, not travel at all.'

Ringg scoffed. 'And suppose you get even better – and come out of warp *before* you go into it? What then, Honourable Old Bald One?'

Rugel only chuckled and did not answer. Vorongil raised his head, smiling, and Bart turned away. *It was not so easy to hold on to his hate for the Lhari....*

There came a day when Bart came on watch to see drawn, worried faces all around him, and when Ringg, followed by his maintenance crew, came into the drives chamber, they threw their levers and gauges on automatic and crowded around his cricket-buzzing apparatus, their crests bobbing in question and dismay. There was a strange, strained sense in the ship, even kind old Rugel snarled. Vorongil seemed to emit sparks as he barked at Ringg. 'You found it?'

'Yes, I found it!' he said. 'In the lining.'

Vorongil used words that were not in Bart's vocabulary, and Ringg held up a hand in protest. 'Captain,' he said, 'I only *locate* metals fatigue – I don't *make* it!'

Vorongil's pale lined face seemed creased in deeper lines than usual. 'There's no help for it,' he said, 'we'll have to put down for repairs. How much time do we have, Ringg?'

'The way I figure, we've got a safety factor of –' he reeled off a string of figures, and Vorongil translated it for the men.

'Which means we've got to touch down for repairs within thirty hours, or risk coming apart at the seams. Bartol, what's the closest listed spaceport?'

Bart dived for the handbooks, programming information, comparative tables of position. The crew drifted his way, and by the time he finished feeding in the strips of information, a row three-deep of Lhari surrounded his chair, including all the ship's officers. Vorongil was right at his shoulder when Bart slipped on his earphones and started decoding the punched strips that fed answers from the computer.

'Nearest port is Cottman Four. It's thirty hours away, almost exactly.'

'I don't like to run it that close,' Vorongil said, and the lines in his face bit deeper and deeper. He swung around to the young, pale-crested Lhari who was head of maintenance. 'Do we need spare parts? Or just general repairs?'

'I'd say – just repairs, sir,' the Lhari said. 'We have plenty of that shielding metal. It's a long job to get through the hulls, but there's nothing we can't fix.'

Vorongil flexed his clawed hands nervously, stretching and retracting them. 'And Cottman's thirty hours. Ringg, you're the fatigue expert. Check it again and see what you say. Can we make it that far?'

Ringg looked pale and there was none of his usual boyish nonsense when he said, 'Captain Vorongil, I swear I wouldn't risk Cottman. We *can't* get through the hull lining in space, and if it goes, we don't have a chance of a hydrogen atom in a tank of halogens. It checked out all right at the last stop, but you know as well as I do what crystallisation does.'

Vorongil's slanted eyebrows made an unbroken line, but he only said, 'That's the word, then, Bartol, find us the closest stop, spaceport or not.'

Bart's hands were shaking with sudden fear. It was a big responsibility, to set them down somewhere at an uncharted stop, off the regular Lhari runs. He checked each digit of the dial that would read their position, fed it into the computer, waited, checked it again while he waited, finally wet his lips and plunged, taking the strip from the computer.

'This small star, called Meristem. It's –' he bit his lip, hard; in his excitement he had almost said *green*. 'It's a type Q, point four, two planets with suitable atmosphere, and in the catalogues it's not classified as inhabited at all.'

'Who owns it?' Vorongil asked.

'I don't have that information on the banks, sir,' Bart said, and Vorongil motioned to the Mentorian woman. So apart were Lhari and human on these ships that Bart had not even had a chance to learn her name. He said, 'Look up a star called Meristem for us,' and the Mentorian woman hurried away. She came back after a moment with the soft-voiced information that it was listed as unexplored but belonging under the Federation of Human Worlds.

Vorongil scowled. 'We don't have much choice,' he said. 'It's only eight hours away; Cottman is thirty, and we don't dare wait that long. Bartol, plot us a warpshift to land us in that system, and on the inner of the two planets, within eight hours. If it's a *green* star, the way they call it, that means low-intensity light and no mercury-vapour installations; we'll be working by dim illumination and we'll need all the light we can get.'

It was the first time that Bart, unaided, had had the responsibility of plotting a warpshift. He checked the coordinates three times, until he felt they were engraved on his brain in fiery letters, before passing them along to Vorongil, and even so, when they went into warpdrive, he felt a stinging sense of dread. '*We could shift into that crazy space and never know where we came out, if I was wrong....*'

But when the stars steadied and took on their old colours, the blaze of a small green sun was steady in the viewport.

'Meristem,' Vorongil said, taking the controls himself with steady hands. 'We're setting down with no control-tower signals and no spaceport repair crews, lads. So let's hope the place is really as uninhabited as that catalogue says. It wouldn't be any fun to set down on a city, or burn up some harmless tribal village – but it's too late to try for Cottman now. So let's hope our luck holds out for a while yet.'

Bart, feeling the minute unsteady trembling some-where in the ship – *imagination*, he told himself, *you can't feel metals fatigue somewhere in the hull lining* – echoed the wish.

He did not know yet what fantastic luck had brought him to Meristem. It was to be a long time before he knew this was the end of his quest, or why.

Chapter Eight

The crews of repairmen were working down in the hold, and the *Swiftwing* was a hell of clanging noise and shuddering heat as, now and then, some piece of the drive units would be started and tested. Maintenance was working overtime, but the rest of the crew, with nothing to do, stood around in the recreation lounge, tried to play games, cursed the heat and dreary dimness through the viewports, and twitched at the boiler-factory racket from the hull.

Towards the end of the third day, the ship's biologist completed his tests and made his report. No signs had been detected of any intelligent life; air, water and gravity were well within tolerable limits. Captain Vorongil, therefore, issued permission for anyone who liked to go outside and have a look around.

No one was happier than Bart at this news. He had a sort of ship-induced claustrophobia; it was good to feel the solid ground under his feet, and the rays of a sun, even a green sun, on his back. Even more, it was good to get away from the constant presence of his shipmates. During the enforced period of idleness, when he could neither bury himself in his duties nor withdraw to his cabin pleading fatigue, he was ill at ease, and their very presence had begun to oppress him unendurably. So many tall thin forms, grey skins, feathery white crests. He knew that from the outside he could not be distinguished from any one of them; he knew that this disguise meant his safety, but just the same he felt the need to get away from them for once. He was always alone; for a change, he felt that he'd like to be alone without other people all around him.

But as he moved away from the ship, Ringg dropped out of a hatchway and hailed him. 'Where are you going?'

'Just for a walk,' Bart said civilly.

Ringg drew a deep breath of weariness. He looked pale, and his clothes were streaked and smudged. 'That sounds good,' he said. 'I've been down in the spaces between the hull and the shielding for three watches now, and if you think it doesn't get hot down there! Hot, and filthy. It feels good to stretch my legs. Mind if I come with you?'

Bart did, but there was nothing he could say except, 'I should think after three watches, you'd want some sleep.'

'What I need is fresh air and a chance to move without banging into somebody's welding torch,' Ringg retorted. 'Anyhow, you shouldn't go rambling around alone on a strange planet. You never know what you're going to run into. How about let's get some food from the rations clerk, so we don't have to hurry back, and do some exploring?'

The sun overhead was a clear bright greenish-gold, high in the sky as they set off lightly laden with what Ringg had persuaded the rations clerk to give them. The shadows fell on the soft grass underfoot, pale, pinkish-yellow with bright violet stalks and puff-ball fruiting bodies. Thin shimmery-white clouds moved in the sky. Bart moved silently, wishing he were alone to enjoy it, but Ringg chattered with undiscourageable friend-liness, and at last, feeling he had to say something, Bart asked, 'How are the repairs coming?'

'Pretty well. We ought to be ready to take off in a few hours more,' Ringg said. 'The reason I was so tied down, there, though – the top man on the other watch got his hand half scorched off, poor fellow. Just luck the same thing didn't happen to me,' he added, reflectively, 'you know that Mentorian – not the one in the drives room, but the young one, the Medic's assistant?'

'I've seen her,' Bart said, suddenly wishing that the Mentorian girl were with him now. It would be nice to hear a human voice, even her tart, scornful one. 'Her name's Meta, I think.'

'Oh, is it a female? Mentorians all look alike to me,' Ringg said, while Bart controlled his face with an effort. 'Be that as it may, she saved me from having the same thing happen. I was just going to pick up a hunk of metal, and she *screamed* at me. Seems they can *see* heat vibrations – she said something about it being red-hot! Wouldn't it be a bit of luck, to be able to see something like that?'

They had reached the foot of a line of tall cliffs, where a steep rockfall divided the plain from the edge of the mountains. At their foot ran a slender rill of water; a widening pool broadened out, with a few slender, drooping gold-leaved trees bending graceful branches into the water. Bart stood, fascinated by the play of green sunlight on the gold, the emerald ripples of the stream, but Ringg cast down his package of food and flung himself full-length on the grass. He sighed, comfortably. 'Feels good!'

'Too comfortable to eat?'

'Not likely,' said Ringg, reaching for a carton.

They munched in companionable silence. 'Look,' said Ringg at last, pointing towards the foot of the cliffs nearby. 'Holes in the rocks. Caves. I'd like to explore them, wouldn't you?'

Bart looked in the direction indicated. 'They look

pretty gloomy to me,' he said. 'And all too likely to have some kind of giant reptiles, dinosaurs or some such thing, living in them.'

Ringg perceptibly shuddered. 'I've noticed that you have a morbid imagination, Bartol. But –' he patted the hilt of his energon-beam gun, 'This will handle anything short of an armour-plated saurian.'

It was Bart's turn to shudder. As part of the uniform, he had been issued with one of the energon-guns, but he had never used it and didn't intend to. He thought of the death of Briscoe, and the memory perceptibly dimmed the lustre of the day. 'Let's not, just now. I'm enjoying the warmth of the sun.'

'It's better than vitamin lamps,' Ringg admitted, 'even if it isn't very bright. I wonder if it has any special properties?'

'I didn't bother to look them up on the chart. I suppose, though, if it was harmful, they wouldn't let us out in it.' Bart wondered, suddenly and worriedly, about the effects of a green sunburn on his chemically-altered skin tone.

'Well, let's enjoy it while we can,' Ringg said, 'because it seems to be clouding over. I shouldn't wonder if it rained after a while.' He yawned. 'I'm getting bored with this voyage. I hate long hops like this one. Are you?'

'A little, maybe.'

Ringg sighed. 'And yet I don't want it to end, because at the end of the voyage, I'll have to fight it out again with my mother and father. *They* want me to settle down and raise a family, instead of shipping out in space. My father owns a hotel, and they wanted me in the family business,' he explained. 'None of our folk have ever been spacemen before. And they can't imagine why, if I have to be a spaceman, I want to ship out to the Second Galaxy. They can't understand that it's the only place

I'm happy, out in space. Living on just one planet would drive me mad. Even when I get old and bald like Rugel, and can't take the warpdrive any more, I'm going to save up enough to own a couple of system ships for planet work. But the family can't see it that way.' He sighed again. 'What about you, Bartol? You've never told me much about yourself. Are you a career man?'

'I guess so. I never thought much about that part of it,' Bart said slowly. Ringg's story had touched him; he had never quite been so aware of how much alike the two races were. Ringg might look like a monster, but he was just a kid who had family trouble and wanted to stay in a line of work he loved.

'What kind of family do you have? Do they understand you?' Ringg asked.

'My mother died when I was young,' Bart said, choosing his words carefully. 'My father always wanted me to be a spaceman, though. He owns a fleet of interplanetary ships... owned them. He's dead too, now.'

Ringg's eyes were bright with sympathy. 'Bad luck,' he said gently. 'Now, of course, I understand why you are always so quiet and - well, standoffish. None of us realised you'd just lost your father. It must have been hard on you - being off *on the drift*, not knowing until afterward that he was gone.' He was silent for a long time. 'Didn't he ever travel between the stars, though? How did he stand it?' Suddenly, Ringg laughed. 'Some of the older generation are like that! When I was in training school, we had a professor - funny old chap, bald as the hull of the *Swiftwing*, taught us astrogation, taught us everything there was to know about it, and he'd never been off the face of the planet! No, not even to one of the moons! He was the supervisor of the student's lodge where I lived at the school, and oh, was he a -' he used a phrase meaning, literally, *a soft piece of cake*. 'His

107

feet may have been buried in the mud, but his head was somewhere in the outer nebulas. He had claw-marks all over his face – he was always trying to button up his throat-piece while he had one eye on the book. We had some of the wildest times,' Ringg reminisced. 'We'd slip away to the town – strictly against the rules, of course – and walk about with capes over our uniforms, and one of us – we used to draw lots – would stay home and sign the book for all twelve of us. You see, he never looked up when we came in, just shoved the wax at us, with his nose in a text on astrogation. So the one who stayed home could walk in, sign the book, walk out the back entrance, and walk in again, twelve times. When twelve had signed, of course, Old Muffin would go up to bed, and late at night the one who stayed would sneak down and let us in!'

Bart laughed heartily. He could almost forget he was not with one of his own schoolmates, so familiar the sound of tricks played on the 'absent-minded professor'. 'I've had professors like that. One of them was the author of a famous textbook on nav-on astrogation, and yet he couldn't count his own change for a robocab!'

Ringg sat up, brushing his hand against his cheek. 'Was that a drop of rain? And the sun's gone in; looks as if we ought to start back, though I hate to leave those caves unexplored.'

Bart bent to gather up the debris of their meal, packing plates and thin paper cups and the remnants (very small) of uneaten food. 'What shall we do about this? Leave it here?'

'Stars above, no!' Ringg exclaimed in horror. 'Let's take it back to the *Swiftwing*. Oh, I've known people who would just leave their junk around, even on a beautiful wild world like this one, but let's not!'

Bart, mildly ashamed of himself, started to stuff the things into one of the sacks. He supposed that was one of the less admirable human traits – willingness to leave things untidy in a deserted place where no one was likely to see them. 'Ouch! What was that?'

Ringg cried out in pain. 'What – it's *hail!*'

The sharp pieces of ice were suddenly raining, pelting, hailing down all around them, splattering the ground with noise, bouncing with a sharp clatter. Ringg ducked and yelled, 'Come on – it's big enough to *flatten* you!'

It looked to Bart as if it were at least golf-ball size and seemed to be getting bigger by the moment. Lightning flashed around them in sudden glare; they ducked their heads and ran.

'Get in under the lee of the cliffs,' Ringg yelled; half blinded by the noise, the glare, the chunks of ice, they held up their hands to protect their faces and struggled on. 'We couldn't possibly make it back to the *Swift* –' his voice broke off in a cry of pain; he slumped forward, pitched to his knees, then slid down and lay still.

'What's the matter?' Bart, arm curved to protect his skull, bent over the fallen Lhari, but Ringg, his forehead bleeding, lay insensible. Bart felt sharp pain in his arm, felt the hail hard as thrown stones raining on his head. Ringg was out cold. *If they stayed in this*, Bart thought despairingly, *they'd both be dead!* He put his hand up to his cheek; a flying fragment of the jagged hail had struck it and it was bleeding. Crouching, trying to duck his head between his shoulders, Bart got his arms under Ringg's armpits and half-carried, half-dragged him under the lee of the cliffs. But the wind flung the hail hard against the rocks; Bart slipped and slid on the thickening layer of ice underfoot, lost his footing, and came down hard, one arm twisted between himself and the cliff. He cried out in pain, uncontrollably, and let Ringg slip from his grasp. The Lhari boy lay like the dead.

Bart bent over him, breathing hard, trying to get his

breath back. The hail was still pelting down, showing no signs of lessening. About five feet away, one of the dark gaps in the cliff showed wide and meancing, but at least, Bart thought, the hail couldn't come in there! He stooped and got hold of Ringg again. A pain like fire went through the wrist he had smashed against the rock; he set his teeth, wondering if it was broken. The effort made him see stars, but he managed somehow to hoist Ringg up again and haul him through the pelting hail towards the yawning gap. It darkened around them, and, blessedly, the pelting of the hail could not reach. Only an occasional light splinter of ice blew with the bitter wind into the mouth of the cave.

Bart laid Ringg down on the floor under the shelter of the rock ceiling. He knelt beside him, and spoke his name, but Ringg just moaned. His forehead was covered with blood.

Bart took one of the paper napkins from the lunch sack and carefully wiped some of it away. His stomach turned at the deep, ugly cut there, which immediately started oozing fresh blood. He pressed the edges of the cut together with the napkin, wondering helplessly how much blood Ringg could lose without danger and if he had concussion. The noise of the hail outside pounded relentlessly on. If he tried to go back to the ship and fetch the Medic for Ringg, doubtless he'd be struck by hail himself – from where he stood, it seemed that the hailstones were getting bigger by the minute!

He put his hand up to his head, discovering that the cut there had already stopped bleeding. He had several minor cuts on his arms, but the worst injury was the wrist. It felt almost as if it were broken; it was certainly badly sprained. Behind him Ringg moaned, but when Bart knelt beside him again he did not answer. Bart could hear only the rushing of wind, the noise of the splattering hail, and a sound of water somewhere . . . *or was that a rustle of scales, a dragging of strange feet?* He looked through the darkness into the depths of the cave, his hand on his shock-beam. He was afraid to turn his back on it.

This is nonsense, he told himself firmly, I'll just walk back there and *see* what is back there. Nothing but rocks, like as not, and maybe a spider or two.

At his belt he had the small flashlamp, excessively bright, that was, like the energon-beam shocker, a part of regulation equipment. He took it out, shining it on the back wall of the cave, then drew a long breath of startlement and for a moment forgot Ringg and his own pain.

For the back wall of the cave was an exquisite fall of crystal! Minerals glowed there, giant crystals, like jewels, crusted with strange lichen-like growths and colours. There were pale blues and greens and shimmering among them, a strangely-coloured crystalline mineral that he had never seen before. It was blue – no, Bart thought, that's just the light, it's more like red – no, it can't be like *both* of them at once, and it isn't really like either. In this light I can't see *what* it looks like. Yet it's a good light, Lhari lights are very bright. It's just a colour I haven't seen –

Ringg moaned again, and Bart, jerking back to attention, ran to him, dropping down at his side.

'What – what happened?' Ringg muttered blurrily.

'You got your head hit. Lie quiet – we're under cover now,' Bart reassured him, 'and I think the hail's stopping.'

Ringg tried to sit upright, but fell weakly back.

'You can't possibly walk back to the *Swiftwing*,' Bart said, worried. 'Lie still. I'll go back and get help.'

The hail had stopped; the ice was slippery underfoot, and it was bitterly cold, but the piled heaps were already melting. Bart wrapped himself in his cloak, glad of its

111

warmth, and struggled back across the meadows that had been so pink and flowery in the sunshine. The loom of the *Swiftwing* in the deserted valley felt like home, and the warmth closing around him, the bright light spilling from the lower hatchway, felt heavenly, but the Second Officer, coming up from the spaces where repair work was still going on, stopped halfway out of the ladder, in consternation.

'Bartol! You're covered in blood! What's the matter? Where's Ringg? Did you two lads get caught out in that hailstorm?'

Quickly Bart explained. 'You'll have to get someone to carry him back, I'm afraid – I'll come with you –'

'You'll do no such thing!' the Second Officer said harshly. 'Look at yourself in a mirror, white-head; you're a mess. I know where the place is – we saw those caves yesterday. I'll get the Medic, if he can leave Karol – you heard about him burning his hand? You go down and have those cuts attended to, and your wrist looked after. That Mentorian girl can do that.'

Bart suddenly heard frightening words in his mind. *Don't break any bones. You won't pass an X-ray.*

'That's an *order*,' the Second Officer snapped. 'If Ringg's under cover, he's safe until we find him; you go down and get those cuts looked after, do you hear me?' He spun on his heel and hurried away, and Bart, his head beginning to hurt, walked slowly up the ladder. His whole arm felt numb and he held it with the other one. He moved slowly, trying to hide the panic he felt.

Could he bluff a Mentorian Medic? Raynor Three had been a Mentorian, and Raynor presumably knew that he would have to face a Medic at some time during the cruise. He went through into the dimmer corridor and into the small infirmary.

The Mentorian girl he had seen before was there, bending over Karol, who lay in a bunk, his hand wrapped thickly in bandages, moaning horribly. She had a hypodermic in her hand; she made the injection, and after a little while, the ghastly moaning quieted and Karol lay still. The Mentorian straightened slowly, and turned, looking at Bart.

'Bartol,' she said, 'You're hurt! Not more burns, I hope?' Her small, pretty, kittenlike face looked pale and drawn. Bart flinched as he looked at Karol's bandaged hand.

'Only a few cuts,' he said in Universal; Meta had spoken in Lhari, but it seemed natural to speak a human tongue to her, and in his weariness and pain he was homesick for the sound of a familiar word.

'The Second Officer just buzzed for the Medic and he's gone,' Meta said, in Universal this time. 'I heard over the intercom that Ringg's been hurt –'

'We were both out in the hailstorm.'

'Well, I can take care of those bruises and cuts,' Meta said crisply. 'Sit down here.'

Bart sat. In her white smock she looked tiny but efficient, and her hands were gentle and cool as she sponged away the blood from his forehead and sprayed it with some cool mint-smelling antiseptic. Bart leaned back, more tired than he knew, half closing his eyes. It was restful to be in the presence of a human being again. He was off his guard for a moment when she asked, 'What ever made you go out in the hail?'

'It wasn't hailing when we went,' Bart said wearily, 'the sun was as bright and green as you could wish for.' He bit the words off, realising he had made a slip, but the girl paid no attention, fastening a clear strip of plastic over the cut, and turning her attention to the lesser cuts on his arms. Then she picked up his wrist.

'I'm afraid this is broken, sir,' she said. 'Better let me X-ray it!'

'No!' Bart's harsh cry was imperative. 'It's all right . . . nothing broken.'

'Does that hurt?'

Bart set his teeth. 'No. It'll be all right, it's just banged up – black and blue, that's all. . . .'

He heard her breath jolt out; her fingers gripped painfully on his wounded wrist. He gasped, but she did not heed. 'Black and blue,' she repeated in a whisper, 'and the sun was nice and *green*. And your eyes – now I look at you, I can see – *what are you?*'

Bart felt himself slip sidewise. He thought he would faint. Terrified, desperate, he looked up at Meta, saw her swallow hard. She blinked.

'You're not . . . *you're not a Lhari*,' she whispered. 'But you look just like one of them –'

Bart nodded, letting his shoulders slump. It was all over. The pain in his wrist blurred everything else, but Meta suddenly realised she was still gripping it, and with a little, gentle cry, cradled the abused wrist in her palm.

'No wonder you didn't want me to X-ray it,' she whispered. Biting her lip, she cast a frightened glance at Karol, unconscious in the bunk. 'No, he can't hear us, I gave him a heavy shot of hypnin, poor fellow.'

'Go ahead,' Bart said bitterly, 'Call your masters!'

Meta went deliberately to the infirmary door and locked it; then turned around to Bart. Her face was white, even the red lips had lost their colour. 'Who are you?' she whispered.

'Does it matter?' Bart asked bitterly.

Shocked comprehension swept over her face.

'You don't think I'd *tell* them,' she whispered. 'Why they might – I don't think so, but they might even *kill* you. I heard talk, in the Procyon port, of a spy that had managed to get through on a Lhari ship. But I didn't know –' she broke off. 'They – you know they'll – make sure I can't – tell anything dangerous to the Lhari, at the end of the voyage,' she whispered faintly. 'But you'll be gone by then, won't you?'

114

'I think so.' He hadn't intended to go further than Antares unless he must. 'But – Meta –' concern for her suddenly swept over him. 'What will they do to you, when they find out you knew – and didn't tell?'

'Why, nothing,' she said, opening her eyes wide. 'The Lhari would never *hurt* anyone, would they?'

He set his mouth grimly. 'I hope you never find out different, girl.'

'Why would they need to?' she said reasonably. 'They could just erase the memory. I never heard of a Lhari harming anyone!'

'I did,' he said, and the terrible memory surged up again. *Briscoe.* And his father was dead....

'Well, they must have done it in self-defence, then,' Meta said forcefully. 'Although – I'm not so sure ...' she wavered, looking at him. 'You look *so* much like a Lhari. I never dreamed – how was it done? Poor fellow, you must be the loneliest man in the whole universe!'

He reached, with his good hand, for hers, instinctively seeking comfort; she flinched away from the touch, and bitterly, he remembered; *he was a monster to this pretty girl....*

Her face softened. 'It looks so real,' she said helplessly, and laid her hand over his. 'Yet, now that I look close, I can see, at the very base of the nails, you have little moons. The Lhari don't... oh, it's terrible!'

There was a noise in the corridor. Dismay and terror swept over Meta's face and she ran to unlock the door.

The Second Officer and the Medic staggered in, carrying Ringg. The Medic said sourly, 'Regular hospital ship we have here!' He glanced at Karol; bent over Ringg.

The Second Officer glanced at Bart and nodded. 'Did you get that wrist looked after?'

Bart saw Meta's hands trembling, but she calmly reached into a drawer, taking out a roll of gauze bandage. 'I X-rayed it,' she said evenly in Lhari. 'It's not broken, it only needs strapping.' And to Bart, 'If you'll hold out your hand, sir....' But he felt her delicate fingers tremble, as she wound the bandage deftly around his wrist.

'How's Ringg?' Bart asked, his voice shaking with strain.

'He'll do,' the Medic said. 'Lucky you got him under cover. He says you dragged him through that hail, and that's how you got hurt. Good boy,' he added dryly, and Bart looked down at the tabletop, to hide what he was sure his face must betray.

'Sure, Bartol saved my life,' Ringg said weakly from the bunk. 'Thanks – shipmate.'

Meta's hand, with a swift hard pressure, lingered on Bart's shoulder briefly, as she cut the bandage. 'There,' she said softly, 'I don't think that will need anything more.' In a whisper, fleetingly, as the Second Officer turned away. 'I didn't dare say it was broken or they'd insist on X-rays. If it hurts I'll give you something for the pain.'

'I think it will do,' Bart said. The tight strapping had made it feel better, but he was dizzy and sick, and when the Medic turned and said brusquely, 'Watch below, Bartol; go and get yourself at least four hours of sleep – that's an order,' he rose and stumbled away with relief.

Safe in his own cabin, door locked, he threw himself down with his head in his arms. He'd come safely through one more terror – one more nightmare. Meta! She had put herself in danger for him. Was there no end to this ceaseless fear? But he couldn't count the danger to her, either.

You're doing this for the stars. It's bigger than your fear... *it's a lot bigger than you are.*

But he was beginning to think it was a lot too big for him.

116

Chapter Nine

The green sun called Meristem lay far behind them in space; Karol's burns had healed and only a few faint purple specks, visible only to Bart, showed the marks of the six stitches which had closed the ugly wound in Ringg's skull. He had neither seen nor spoken to the Mentorian girl Meta again alone. His wrist, after a few days of nightmarish pain when he tried to bend it or pick up anything heavy, had healed. Two more warpdrive shifts through space, two Lhari spaceports, and two more stops had taken them far, far out to the rim of the known Galaxy, and now the great crimson coal of Antares, like an enormous red eye, burned in their viewports as they traversed the outer edge of the enormous planetary system of that enormous star.

Antares had twelve planets, the outermost of which – far away now, at the furthest point of its orbit from the point of the *Swiftwing*'s entry into the system – was a small captive sun; no larger than the planet Earth, it made Antares technically into a double star, revolving every ninety years around its huge primary. Small as it was, it was blazingly brilliant blue-white, and had a tiny planet of its own, and Bart knew that after their stop on the inner planet of Antares Seven, where the trading centre and spaceport were located, they would make a careful orbit around the great sun and land on this tiny planetoid before leaving the system for their unknown destination in the Lhari worlds.

As Bart watched Antares growing in the viewport, he felt a variety of emotions. On the one hand he was glad that his voyage in secrecy was over. Here he would contact those men who would have joined his father, if his father had lived. And after that – what? Would they return him to human form and send him back to Vega? Or would they – unthinkably – demand that he go on, into the Lhari Galaxy? What would he say if they did? Bart did not know. At one moment he longed for the company of his own kind; at another, watching the flame of Antares blurring the lesser stars, he ached to think that this voyage between the stars must end so soon. He had really learned nothing, except that humans *could* survive warpdrive with neither coldsleep nor drugs.

They made planetfall at the largest Lhari spaceport he had yet seen, almost as big as a city on Earth. As always, the Second Officer went immediately to the Message Bureau to pick up any exchanged mail that had been left for scheduled ships; when he came back with the *Swiftwing*'s mail packet, he looked startled and amused.

'So you're not quite the orphan we thought, Bartol! A letter has finally reached you!'

Bart took it, his heart suddenly pounding, and walked away through the groups of officers and crew eagerly debating how they would spend their port leave. He shut himself in his cabin to read it – Ringg, fortunately, was on watch. He knew what it would be.

It was written in Lhari letters, addressed simply to Bartol of the *Swiftwing*, but it was on the letterhead of the Eight Colours Corporation. It contained only an address and a time . . . and the time was when he was on watch aboard!

For a moment he felt absolute frustration, combined

with a sort of relief. Then common sense came to his help. He *had* to get to that address at that time; if he couldn't get leave, he had to go without it! But he wasn't quite ready to draw that much attention to himself yet!

He had never asked Ringg for a favour before. He hunted up the watch schedules, found that Ringg's port leave was scheduled at the time he was on watch, and asked the young Lhari to change watches with him. Since watch when the ship was in port was a simple matter of guard duty and supervising loading crews, Ringg agreed with immediate, cheerful pleasure. 'Sure thing! Glad to do it for you! Got a girl in the port, hey?'

Bart managed a sheepish grin, but the thought set off an almost hysterical desire to laugh. He couldn't even tell a Lhari girl to look at her, any more than Ringg had known by sight that Meta was a female human! 'No, just a - an old friend of my father's.'

'Well, you go right ahead. I'll fix it up with Rugel. Don't you worry about it,' Ringg assured him.

Bart's next move was to slip away to the Mentorians' quarters and borrow a cloak from Meta. She did not ask what he wanted it for, and looked up at him, rather helplessly, when he would have told her.

'Don't tell me anything,' she whispered, 'I'm afraid to know.' Her eyes looked round and scared, and Bart wished he could comfort her, but he knew she would shrink away from him, repelled and horrified by his Lhari skin, hair, claws. He swallowed hard, trying to control his loneliness, and said only, 'Thank you, Meta. I'll make sure it doesn't get you into trouble, whatever happens.'

'I don't care,' she said suddenly, surprisingly, and reached out for his hand, gripping it hard in her own dainty one. 'Bartol - be careful,' she whispered, then stopping, '*Bartol* - that's a Lhari name, what's your real name?'

'Bart. Bart Steele.'

'Good luck – Bart,' she whispered, and tears stood in her eyes. 'Be careful.'

With the blue cloak folded around his face, half concealing his Lhari features, hands tucked into the slits at the side, Bart felt like himself for the first time in many months. And as the strange crimson twilight folded down across the streets, laden with strange spicy smells and strange little fragrant gusts of wind, he almost savoured the sense of being a conspirator, playing for high stakes in the network of intrigue between the stars. He was off on an adventure, and it was new and strange, and he meant to enjoy it.

He built a comfortable fantasy of what the unknown conspirators might say when they knew that he, a mere youngster, had done what only one other human being had ever done – travelled, awake and aware, on a Lhari ship through warpdrive. That information, at least, he told himself, would be worth something. And then he sobered a little, realising that, after all, his father had died in this work – and it was the news of his father's death that he was bringing.

The address he had been given was not far from the spaceport; a lavish estate, across a gleaming lake that shimmered red, violet, indigo in the red sunset, surrounded by a low wall of what looked like purple glass. At what appeared to be a sort of gatehouse, a withered little man stopped him, and glared suspiciously at the Lhari, and Bart did not dare to speak in his own voice. He said in Universal, 'My name is Bartol. I believe I'm expected.'

The man scowled sceptically and punched some sort of intercom device. Bart did not hear what he said, but he looked surprised when he looked up. 'Right, Mister Montano,' he said into the speaker, and jerked his head at Bart. 'Go on up.' He pressed a button and a gap slid open in the purple wall. Bart, moving slowly through the gate, feeling his cloak fall and swing out heavily behind him as he moved in the curiously-muscled step of the Lhari, felt the man's curious eyes boring into his back. He forced himself to walk with slow dignity, but he wanted to run.

Up the path. Up a low flight of gleaming black marble stairs. A door swung open and shut again, closing out the red sunset, and letting him into a room that seemed dim after months of Lhari lights. There were three men in the room, but his eyes were immediately drawn to one, who was standing against an old-fashioned fireplace.

He was very tall, and quite thin, and his hair was snow white, though he did not look old. Bart's first, incongruous thought was, *he* would make a better Lhari than I did! But the blazing eyes were dark and inquisitive, and his firm, commanding step forward told Bart at once that this man was in charge; the others mere associates.

'You are Bartol?'

'That's right.'

Suddenly the white-haired man was directly in front of him, holding out his hand as if to shake hands. Bart took it – and found himself instantly gripped in a judo hold, the other two men leaped into place behind him. They felt all over his body, not gently.

'No weapons,' said one.

'Listen here –' Bart began.

'Save it. If you're the right person you'll understand,' said the tall man. 'If you're the wrong one, you won't have much time to resent it. A very simple test. What colour is that?' He pointed to a low divan.

'Green.'

'And that?'

'Darker green, with a gold and red figure.'

The men released him, and the white-haired one smiled. 'So you actually did it, Steele! I thought for certain the code message was a fake!' He stepped back and looked Bart over from head to foot, whistling. 'Raynor Three must be a genius! Claws and everything! What a devil of a risk to take, though! I admit, I wouldn't do it!'

'You know my name,' Bart said, 'but who are you?'

Suspicion came back into the dark eyes. 'Does that Mentorian cloak mean they've gotten to you? Lost your memory?'

'No,' said Bart, 'it's simpler than that. I'm not Rupert Steele. I'm –' his voice caught, 'I'm his son.'

The man looked startled and shocked. He said softly, 'I suppose that means Rupert is dead. Dead! It came a little before he expected it, then. So you're Bart.' He sighed. 'My name's Montano. This is Hedrick –' he gestured to a short, fat man, obviously from Aldebaran, 'and I suppose you'd recognise Raynor Two.'

Bart blinked. It was surprising to see the grim face of Raynor One, and the identical-but-different, kindly face of Raynor Three, on still another man. Raynor Two looked hard and dangerous.

'But sit down,' Montano said with a wave of his hand, 'make yourself comfortable!'

Hedrick relieved Bart of his cloak; Raynor Two put a cup of some hot steaming drink in his hand, passed him a tray of small hot fried things that tasted crisp and delicious. Bart relaxed in the admiring looks of the two men, answering their questions. How old? Only seventeen? And you came all alone on a Lhari ship – working your way as an Astrogator? It was almost dangerously like the fantasy he had invented. But Montano stood watching, with a frown between his thick white eyebrows, and interrupted at last, not gently.

'All right, this isn't a party and we haven't all night. I don't suppose Bart has, either. That's enough time wasted. Since you walked into this, young Steele, I take it you know what's going on and what risks are involved – what we're intending to do next?'

Bart shook his head. 'No. Raynor Three wanted to send me, as a passenger, just to call off your plans –'

'That sounds like Three,' interrupted Raynor Two. 'Entirely too squeamish!'

Montano said irritably, 'Shut up, Two. We couldn't have done anything without a man on the *Swiftwing*, and you know it – and we can't get to the Mentorians. How many Mentorians on the ship, Bart?'

'Only three. Two in the drives room, one medical assistant.'

'Good, that means they don't have a lot of special gadgets. Now I suppose you've found out, on the *Swiftwing*, about *Lharillis*?'

'Not by that name.'

'Your next stop. The planetoid of the little captive sun.'

'Oh. Yes.'

'You know about it? No, I can tell that you don't. Well, first of all, that planetoid is the first spot the Lhari visited in this galaxy. Before they met the Mentorians, even, they stopped there. They didn't build a spaceport, though. The place is utterly uninhabited – just bare rock. It's an inferno of light from that little blue-white sun, so of course they love it – it's just like home to them. They were going to build a station there, but when they found out that the inner planets of Antares proper were inhabited, they put the spaceport here so they'd have a better chance at trade.' Montano's mouth twisted. 'Besides, humans are uncomfortable on that little hunk of rock they call Lharillis. And the Lhari would *never* make humans uncomfortable!' He scowled fiercely.

'Well, without going into a lot of politics, the Lhari wanted to acquire that little world, but we threatened a war over it. The Lhari don't get *anything* where we can't watch them and inspect it! We went all over the planetoid making sure there were no rare minerals there, and finally leased it to them, a century at a time. They mine the place for some kind of powdered lubricant that's better than graphite, with robot machinery – no one is stationed there permanently – and every time a ship comes into this system they stop there, although there's nothing there but a landing field, some concrete bunkers filled up with robot machinery for mining, and some kind of a monument. They'll stop there on the way out of the system, and that's where you come in.'

'Me?'

'Not you alone,' Montano said, 'but you're aboard the Lhari ship. Somehow, you'll have to manage to put their radiation counter out of commission.'

He turned, took a chart from a drawer; spread it out on a tabletop. 'The simplest way,' he said, 'would be to cut these two wires. You see, Bart – when the Lhari land, one of our ships is going to be there, hidden. Waiting for them.'

'And if I put the counter out of order –'

'Then they won't be able to detect us approaching and landing. Our plan is to take over the Lhari ship – they must have full records aboard of where they go for their special fuel catalyst.'

Bart whistled. 'But what about the crew? Won't they defend it? You can't fight the Lhari, with their energon-beam guns!'

Montano's face was calm, perfectly quiet. 'We don't intend to fight them at all. We would certainly lose such a battle – our weapons of that sort are not nearly as good,' he said. 'We're not even going to attempt it.'

124

He handed Bart a small strip of pale-yellow plastic.

'Take this,' he said. 'Keep it out of sight from the Mentorians – the Lhari won't be able to see the colour of it, so it won't matter, but keep your eyes on it. When it turns orange, you'd better take cover.'

'What is it?'

'Radiation-exposure film,' Montano said. 'It's exactly as sensitive to radiation as you are. When it starts to turn orange, it's picking up radiation, and when it turns red – well, you won't see it turn. If you're aboard the ship, get into the drive chambers – they're lead-lined – and you'll be safe there. If you're out on the surface, you'll be all right in one of the concrete bunkers where they keep the mining machinery. But get under cover before it turns very deep orange, because not long after that, every Lhari of them will be stone cold dead.'

Bart let the strip of plastic drop from his fingers, staring in disbelief at Montano's calm, cruel face. 'Kill them? Kill a whole *shipload* of them? That's – that's –' he couldn't find a word, and shook his head helplessly. 'You can't mean it!'

'I told you he'd been around the Lhari too long,' said Hedrick.

'Shut up,' Montano said, 'I told you, he's only a kid. He doesn't realise.' He came over to Bart. 'Look here, don't you understand, this is WAR?'

'We're *not* at war with the Lhari! We have a treaty of trade and peace with them!' Bart protested furiously.

'The Federation has – because they don't dare do anything else,' Montano said furiously, 'but there are some of us who dare to *do* something – who aren't going to sit and *die*, sit and let them strangle all humanity, hold them down! It's war, just the same, Bart, and it's a war for economic survival. Do you suppose the Lhari would hesitate to kill any of us, or all of us, if we did anything to hurt their monopoly of star travel?'

125

Bart hesitated, and Montano pressed his advantage.

'I suppose they told you about young Briscoe? How the Lhari hunted him down –'

'But how do we know that was Lhari policy and not just some fanatic?' Bart asked suddenly. He thought of the death of the elder Briscoe and, as always, he shivered with the horror of it, but for the first time it occurred to him that Briscoe had provoked his own death. He had physically attacked the Lhari, threatened them – forced them to shoot him down in self-defence.

'I've been on board with them for months. They aren't – wanton murderers.'

Raynor Two made a derisive sound. 'Sounds like the Mentorians have got to him, too!'

Hedrick growled. 'Why do we waste time arguing with this young punk? Listen, young Steele, you'll do as you're told, unless you want to stay Lhari for the rest of your life. Who said you had the right to question or pass judgment on our orders?'

'Be still, both of you,' Montano ordered. 'He may be young, but he's reliable.' There was a persuasive charm, very hard to resist in his voice. He came and laid his arm around Bart's shoulder. 'Bart, I know how you feel. You've been with them, it seems to you that they're your comrades and friends. But that's only because they think you're one of themselves. You can trust us, can't you? You're Rupert Steele's son – you'll do what your father intended, won't you?' The persuasive, kindly voice softened. 'Bart, don't waste his life's work. If you fail us now, there may not be another chance like this for years – maybe not in our lifetime!'

'I don't know what to do,' Bart said helplessly, and dropped his head in his hands.

Kill a whole shipload of Lhari – innocent traders! Bald, funny old Rugel, stern Vorongil, his friend Ringg –

Or was it true, what Montano said – that they

wouldn't hesitate to kill –

'I don't know what to do,' he repeated, and Montano said, very gently, 'It's hard to know, isn't it? But trust us, Bart. You're human, too – you're human,' he repeated, his arm around Bart's shoulders.

Bart looked round at the men in the room waiting for his decision. Yes, he was human. . . .

Montano saw the moment when he weakened. He said softly, almost tenderly, 'You've had the chance to do what the Lhari are keeping us from doing – you've even seen space between the stars. Your father wanted that for all of us, but he never got it. Won't you – give it to your own people? You couldn't side with the Lhari against men – could you? Could a son of Rupert Steele do that?'

Bart shut his eyes. The struggle seemed unbearable, but as he looked up, he felt something snap inside him. No, he couldn't take their part against his own people.

'All right,' he said at last, thickly, 'I'll do it.'

When he left Montano's house, half an hour later, he had the details of the plan, had memorised the location of the device he was to put out of order, and had accepted, from Montano, a pair of special dark contact lenses. 'It's a hellish inferno of light out there,' Montano warned him. 'I know you're half Mentorian, but they don't even take their Mentorians out there. They're proud of saying no human foot has ever touched Lharillis – a fat lot they know about it! They put their Mentorians in coldsleep before they touch down there. Better wear these.'

When he got back to the Lhari spaceport, Ringg hailed him. 'Hey there, where have you been? Vorongil came down and gave us all an off-watch, and I hunted the whole port over for you! If we don't stick together on a planet crawling with aliens, how'll we manage?'

127

'I was busy,' Bart said shortly.

'I know, with your father's old friend. But how long did that take? Anyhow, come along, the place is jumping,' Ringg urged. 'I wouldn't join the party until you came – what's a pal for anyhow?'

Bart brushed by him without speaking. 'I'm not going down to the port,' he said, disregarding Ringg's surprised stare, and went up the ramp of the *Swiftwing*. He reached his own bunk and flung himself down, torn in two.

Ringg was his friend. Ringg liked him! He, himself, sometimes forgot for hours at a time that he was not with some friend of his own schooldays, like Tom. And if he did what Montano wanted, Ringg would die!

He became aware that Ringg had followed him and was standing in the cabin door, staring at him. 'Bartol, is something the matter? Is there anything I can do? Have you had more bad news?'

Bart's torn nerves snapped. He raised his head and yelled at Ringg. 'Yes, there is something! You can quit following me around and just let me alone for a change!'

Ringg took a step backward. Then he said, very softly, 'Suit yourself, Bartol. Sorry,' and noiselessly, his white crest held high, he glided away. Bart's resolve hardened. Loneliness had done odd things to him – thinking of Ringg, a Lhari, one of the freaks who had killed his father, as a friend! Yet if they knew who he was, they would turn on him – hunt him down as they'd hunted Briscoe, as they'd hunted his father, as they'd hounded him from Earth to Procyon! He put his scruples aside. He'd made up his mind.

They could all die. What did he care? He was human – that was what mattered – and he was going to be loyal to his own kind.

But although he thought he had settled all the conflict in

128

his mind, he found that it returned, again and again, when he was lying in his bunk, or when he stood in the dome and watched the stars, while they moved through the Antares system under the slow speed-of-light drive, towards the captive sun and the tiny planet Lharillis.

It's in my power to give this to all men. . . .

Should a few Lhari stand in his way.

He lay in his bunk brooding, thinking of death, staring at the yellow radiation badge. *If you fail, it won't be in our lifetime.* He'd have to go back to little things, to the little ships that hauled piddling cargo between little planets, while all the grandeur of the stars belonged to the Lhari. And if he succeeded, Vega Interplanet could spread from star to star, a mighty memorial to Rupert Steele. . .

He brooded, hardly speaking to Ringg, wrapped in silence as he went through his routine watches at the computer. One day Vorongil sent for him.

'Bartol,' he said, and his voice was not unkind, 'you and Ringg have always been good friends, so don't be angry about this. He's worried about you – says you spend all your spare time in your bunk growling at him. Is there anything the matter, white-head? Sometimes an old head can make light of problems that would crush a young crest. Want to talk about it?'

He sounded so concerned, so – the word struck Bart with hysterical humour – so *fatherly*, that Bart wanted insanely to laugh and to cry. Instead he muttered, 'Ringg should mind his own business.'

'But it's not like that,' Vorongil said. 'Look, the *Swiftwing*'s a world, young fellow, and a small one. If one being in that world is unhappy, it affects everyone. Do you know the writings of Mesarkin of Khaz? *If a hair is ruffled on my brother's crest, can I sleep untroubled?*'

Bart had an absurd, painful impulse to blurt out the incredible truth to Vorongil, and try to get the old captain to see what he was doing. And after that – what? He needn't give up anything. He was a Mentorian; he could work with them. . . .

But fear held him silent. Suppose they turned on him? He was alone, one small human in a ship of Lhari, and all his life he had heard nothing but prejudice. His mother had trusted and liked the Lhari – but she was a Mentorian, one of the special pets of the Lhari. No, he had no choice.

But could he let Vorongil die?

He had to do what Montano said. It was his only chance to get back his human form. . . .

Vorongil was looking at him, deep lines drawn between his brows, and Bart mumbled, 'It's really nothing, Honourable Bald One. I had bad news on Antares.'

'I suppose you're pining for home, then,' Vorongil said. 'Well, it won't be long now. Lharillis – then the long jump, and then we're back in familiar territory.'

The glare of the captive sun grew and grew, and Bart's fear and dread grew, too. He had, as yet, had no chance to put the radiation counter out of order. Sometimes, in sleepless nights, it seemed that would be the best way to handle it – just let it go. But then the Lhari would detect Montano's ship, and they would kill Montano and his men –

Did he believe that?

He had to believe it. It was the only way he could justify what he was doing.

The radiation apparatus was behind a panel in the drives chamber, and Bart lay awake at night trying to figure out a way to get to it undetected. He was seldom alone on watch for more than a minute or two. He almost wished he would never have a chance. It would solve so many problems.

And then it came, as so many chances do when one no

longer wants them. The Second Officer, in charge of the watches on these routine inside-system flights, came to him and said, 'Bartol, old Rugel's sick – not fit to be on his feet. Do you think you can hold down the panels tonight, if I drop in and give you a hand now and then?'

'I think so,' Bart said, carefully not overemphasising it. The Second Officer, by routine, spent half of his time in the drives chamber where they were, and half down on the Maintenance Decks, travelling between the two about once in three-quarters of an hour.

Bart timed the trip twice with his chron; on the Second Officer's third absence, he ripped open the panel, located the wires, and hesitated; he didn't quite dare cut them outright. Someone might notice, even though this radiation detector was used only inside planetary fields; out in space, the cosmic-ray analyser was used.

He jerked one wire loose, frayed the other with a sharp claw until it was almost in shreds and would break with the first touch, pulled at another until it was not making full contact. He supposed that it wouldn't give way until someone put power to it. He closed the panel and brushed dust over it, and when the Second Officer returned, he was back at his own station.

As Antares fell towards them in the visionport, he found himself worrying about the Mentorians. They would be in coldsleep, presumably in a safe part of the ship, or Montano would have made provision for them. Still, he wished there was some way to warn Meta. He had returned her cloak to her quarters, careful to do it when he knew she was not there; he told himself that if he were seen talking to her, it would endanger them both. Yet he longed to consult with her. If he could only tell her . . .

But she was a Mentorian. There was that.

He was not on watch the day when they came into the

planetary field of Lharillis, but when he came on watch just before final deceleration and landing, he knew at once that the trouble in the radiation counter had been discovered; the panel was hanging open, the exposed wires pulled out, and Ringg was facing old Rugel, shouting.

'Listen, Baldy, I won't have you accusing me of scamping or going light on my work! I tell you, I checked those wires five periods ago, and they were perfectly all right then. Tell me who's going to be opening the panels in here anyhow?'

'No, no,' old Rugel said patiently, 'I'm not accusing you of anything only maybe being careless, young Ringg. You poke with those buzzing instruments and things of yours, maybe one time you tear loose some wires.'

'Well, I didn't,' Ringg shouted.

'Nobody opens the panels but you!'

Ringg swung around to Bart. 'Did you ever see such nerve as the old guy has! My business is *fixing* things, not messing them up!'

Bart remembered he wasn't supposed to know what had happened. 'What's going on?'

'Why, that unprintable radiation detector's haywire,' Rugel growled, 'and Ringg here is supposed to be responsible –'

'Responsible nothing! I checked it!'

Rugel said, placatingly, 'Oh well, we can fix it when we land, it's not as if this were a planet with radioisotopes floating around on it. This is Lharillis, remember? If it were the landing gear, now –'

But Ringg was not to be placated. 'It's a matter of my professional competence and reputation!'

'Forget it,' Bart said. 'If Rugel's not sore, what does it matter? You probably skipped it when you were checking, and it rusted or something.'

'No,' Ringg said truculently, 'I've got it checked off in my daybook, I tell you. Somebody was probably blundering around, opening panels where they had no business to, and tore out the wires by accident, then was too sneaky to admit it and get it fixed like a decent person would do!'

'No, they didn't either,' Rugel said angrily, 'because either Vorongil's down here or I am, every hour in the day and I tell you nobody's *opened* that panel without one of us seeing!'

'And nothing gets by Vorongil, that's for sure,' said the Second Officer placatingly. 'You too, Rugel. Bartol was alone on watch one night, but why would *he* get into the panels?'

Bart felt a cold chill down his spine, but Ringg turned to him.

'Look – Bart, did you? By mistake maybe, thinking it was something else? If you did, it won't count against you on your credits, but it's my job and it means a black mark for me. If you did, own up – huh? Alone on watch and not wanting to ask the officer for something, maybe?'

'No,' Bart flung back, tautly, 'why go through this because you can't admit you did something stupid once?'

'I resent that!' Ringg stepped angrily towards him, his hands raised menacingly, 'I've taken a lot from you, but when you start questioning my competence –' he started to seize Bart's shoulder; Bart moved to throw him off, clenched his fists, hurt his hand with his claw, remembered where he was, just as Ringg's outthrust claws suddenly raked down his cheek. In pure reflex his own claws shot out. *Not a fistfight* – a clawfight, reeled in his mind as they clinched, closed, slipped back – he felt his claws rake flesh, saw a thin white line appear on Ringg's forearm, bright red blood bursting out. Then

133

Rugel's arms were restraining him, and the Second Officer was holding the struggling Ringg, and Vorongil, leaping into the room, took in the scene with one blistering glare.

For the first time, Bart saw Vorongil's famous temper in action. The tongue-lashing the Captain gave them both taxed his knowledge of Lhari to the uttermost – he was glad he did not understand quite all of it. At the end he felt as if he'd rather Ringg's claws had laid him bare to the bone and bleeding than to have Vorongil calling them half-fledged hairless nestlings, showing their claws like babies instead of doing men's work.

'So someone forgot the panel or damaged the panel by mistake – no, not a word, either of you,' he commanded as Ringg's head came up proudly. 'I don't care who did what! Twenty years ago I could have had you both beaten for this! And I warn you if there is any more on this ship, the one who does it can try claws with me!' He looked both ugly and dangerous. 'I thought better of you both! Now get below, you squalling white-headed nestlings – both of you! Let me not see either of your faces again before we land!'

As they went along the corridor, Ringg turned to Bart, apology and chagrin on his face, but Bart kept his eyes firmly averted. He wanted to make up with Ringg – but it was easier this way, without the pretence of friendship.

It wouldn't last long now. . . .

The light grew more and more intense; Bart had never known anything like it. He was glad to slip away and put the dark contact lenses into his eyes. A quick glance into a mirror showed him that it made his eyes look enormous, with dilated pupils; he hoped none of the Lhari would notice anything. Then he thought, harshly; none of them would live long enough for it to matter. His arm smarted, and he did not speak to Ringg during the long angle of deceleration.

They touched down, the intercom in the ship ordered all crew members to the hatchway, and Bart lingered a moment after Ringg, pinning the badge in the fold of his cloak. A spasm of fear threatened to overwhelm him again, and a nightmarish loneliness and revulsion for his own Lhari form. He felt agonisingly homesick for his own familiar face. He felt it was more than he could manage, to step out into that corridor full of Lhari, assembled to visit the monument of their proud race.

But he managed it, mentally kicking himself into the corridor behind Ringg. The other youngster, always cheerful, glanced at Bart and murmured irreverently, 'I see Old Baldy's going to hike out with us – and the Captain, too!'

The hatch opened. Even accustomed, as he was, to Lhari lights, Bart squeezed his eyes shut for a moment at the blue-white brilliance that assaulted them now; then, opening his slitted eyelids cautiously, he found that he could see perfectly well.

A weirdly desolate scene stretched away before them. Bare burning sand, strewn with curiously coloured rocks, lay piled about in strange chaos – or so it seemed; then he realised there was an odd, but perceptible geometry to their arrangement; they lay showing alternate crystal and opaque faces. Old Rugel noted his look of surprise.

'Never been here before?'

'No, the ship I was on came in from the other angle.'

'That's right, you were working into the Polaris run. Well, those aren't true rocks, but living creatures of a sort. The crystals are alive; the opaque faces are lichens that have something like chlorophyll and can make their food from air and sunlight. The rocks and lichens live in symbiosis. They have intelligence of a sort, but fortunately they don't mind us, or our automatic mining machinery. Every time, though, we find some new lichen that's trying to set up a symbiote-cycle with the concrete of our bunkers!'

'And every time,' Ringg said cheerily, 'somebody – usually me – has to see about having them scraped down and repainted. Maybe some day I'll find a paint the lichens don't like the taste of!'

'Going to explore with Ringg?' Rugel asked, and Ringg always ready to let bygones be bygones, grinned and said, 'Sure!' Bart could not face him:

Remember his friendliness isn't for you, Bart Steele, it's for a Lhari named Bartol!

You Judas, you'd let him go to his death....

Vorongil stopped and said, 'This your first time here, young Bartol? How would you like to visit the monument with me? You can see the machinery on the way back.'

Relieved at not having to go with Ringg, he followed the Captain, falling into step beside him. They moved in silence away from the other Lhari along the smooth-faced stone path.

'The crystal creatures made this road,' Vorongil said at last. 'I think they read minds a little. There used to be a very messy, rocky desert here, and we used to have to scrabble and scratch our way to the monument, though it was always easier coming back. then one day a ship – not mine – touched down and discovered that there was a beautiful smooth road leading up to the monument. And the lichens never touch that stone – but you probably had all this in school.'

Bart nodded noncommittally, he hoped as befitted a young Lhari on a walk with his captain. He wished Vorongil did not sound so kind. 'Excited, Bartol?'

'No – no, sir. Why?'

'Eyes look a bit odd. It's this light, most likely. But who could blame you for being excited? I never come here without remembering Rhazon and his crew on that long jump. The longest any Lhari captain ever made. A blind leap in the dark, remember, Bartol. Through the dark, through the void, with his own crew cursing him for taking the chance. No one had ever crossed between galaxies – and remember, they were using the Ancient Maths!' He paused, and Bart said through a catch of breath. 'Quite an achievement.' His badge still looked reassuringly yellow.

'You young people have no sense of wonder,' Vorongil said. 'Not that I blame you, you can't realise what it was like in those days. Oh, we'd had star travel for centuries, we were beginning to stagnate! And now look at us! Oh, they derided Rhazon – said that even if he did find anyone, any other race, they'd be monsters with whom we could never communicate! But here we have a whole new galaxy for peaceful trade, a new mathematics that takes all the hazard out of space travel, our Mentorian friends and allies –' he smiled. 'Don't tell the High Council on me, but I think they deserve a lot more credit that most Lhari care to give them. Between ourselves, I think the next Search may see it that way.'

Vorongil paused. 'Here's the monument.'

It lay between crystal columns, tall, of blue pale sandstone, with letters in deep shadow of such contrast that the Lhari could read them: a high, sheer, imposing stele. Vorongil read the words slowly aloud in the musical Lhari language:

*Here, with thanks to Those who Watch the Great
Night, I, Rhazon of Nedrun, raise a stone of memory.
Here we first touch the new worlds. Let us never again
fear to face the unknown, trusting that the Mind of All
Knowledge still has many surprises in store for all the living.*

He repeated the words, gently. 'Let us never fear to face the unknown,' he murmured. 'That awful blind leap in the darkness. I think I admire courage more than anything there is, Bartol. Who else could have dared it? Doesn't it make you proud to be a Lhari?'

Bart had felt profoundly moved; now he snapped back to awareness of who he was and what he was doing. So only the Lhari had courage? *Life has surprises, all right, Captain,* he thought grimly.

He glanced down at the badge strip of plastic on his arm. It began to tinge faint orange as he looked, and a chill of fear went over him. He had to get away somehow! Get to cover!

He looked round and his fear was almost driven from his mind.

'Captain, the rocks! They're moving!'

Vorongil said, unruffled, 'Why, so they are. They do, you know; they have intelligence of a sort. Though I've never actually seen them move before; I know they shift places overnight. I wonder what's going on?' They were edging back, the path widening and changing. 'Oh, well, maybe they're going to do some more landscaping for us. I once knew a captain who swore they could read his mind.'

Bart saw the slow, inexorable deepening of his badge, he *had* to get away. He tensed, impatient; gripped by fists of panic. Plain simple fear of death; somewhere on this world, Montano and his men were setting up their lethal radiations....

Think of this: a Lhari ship of our own to study, to know how it works, to see the Catalyst and synthesise it and find out where it comes from, to read their records and star routes. Now we know we can use it without dying in the warpdrive....

Think of this: to be human again, yet to travel the stars with men of his own race!

It's worth a few deaths!

Even Vorongil? Standing here, talking to him, he might – *say it! You talked to him as if he'd been your Father! Oh, Dad, Dad, what would you do?*

His voice was steady, through tight throat, as he looked at Vorongil.

'It's very good of you to show me all this, sir, but the other men will call me a slacker; hadn't I better get to a work detail?'

'Hm, maybe so, white-head,' Vorongil said. 'Let me see – well, down this way is the last row of bunkers,' he said. 'Down there. See the humps? You can check inside to see if they're full or empty and save us the trouble of exploring if they're all empty. Have a look round inside if you care to – the robot machinery's interesting.'

Bart tensed; he had wondered how he'd get hidden inside, but he asked, 'Not locked?'

'Locked?' The old Lhari's short, yellowed crest bobbed in surprise. 'Why?' Who ever comes here but our ships? And what would we do with the stuff but take it back with us? Why locked? You've been on the drift too long – among those thieving humans! It's time you got back to live among decent folk again. Well, go along.'

The sting of the words stiffened Bart as he took his leave. The colour of the badge seemed deeper orange. . . .

When it's red, you're dead.

It's true. The Lhari don't steal. They don't even seem to understand dishonesty.

But they lied – lied to us all. . . .

Knowing what we were like, maybe! That we'd steal their ships, their secrets, their lives!

The deepening colour of the badge seemed the one visible thing in a strange glaring world. He walked along the row of bunkers; he realised he need not check if

139

they were full or empty – the Lhari wouldn't live long enough to harvest their better-than-graphite lubricant. They'd be dead.

Dead. Ringg, his friend, his shipmate. Crusty old Rugel. Vorongil. . . .

Did Vorongil have a son?

My father is dead. Will Vorongil's son wait for his father to come back from space, and never see him again. . . .

The last bunker was empty. He looked at his orange badge, and stepped inside, heart pounding so loudly he thought it was an external sound . . . it *was* an external sound. A step.

'Don't move one step,' said a voice in Universal, and Bart froze, trembling. He looked cautiously around.

Montano stood there, space-suited, his head bare, dark contact lenses blurring his eyes. And in his hand a drawn blaster was held level – trained at Bart's heart.

Chapter Ten

After the first moment of unquenchable panic, Bart realised the truth, Montano could not tell him from a Lhari. He remained motionless, saying quietly, 'It's me, Montano – Bart Steele.'

The man lowered his weapon and put it away. 'You nearly got yourself cut down,' he said. 'Did you make it all right?' He crossed behind Bart, inspecting the fastening of the bunker. 'Funny you should choose this one to hide out in.'

'It wouldn't have been so funny if two or three of the other Lhari had been with me,' Bart said. Now that Montano had put the weapon away and the danger was over, he was shaking again.

'It's just luck I didn't shoot you first and ask questions afterwards,' Montano said, drew a deep breath and sat down on the concrete floor. 'Anyway, we're safe in here. We've got about half an hour before the radiation will reach lethal intensity. It has a very short half-life, though; only about twelve minutes. If we spend an hour in here, we'll be safe enough. Did you have any trouble putting the radiation counter out of commission?'

'None to speak of,' Bart said, not inclined to talk.

So in half an hour they would all be dead. Ringg, Rugel, Captain Vorongil. Two dozen Lhari, all dead so that Montano could have a Lhari ship to play with.

And what then? More killing, more murder? Would

Montano start killing everyone who tried to get the secret of the drive from him? The Lhari had the stardrive; maybe it belonged to them, maybe not, maybe humans had a right to have it too, but this wasn't the right way. Maybe they didn't deserve it.

He turned to look at Montano. The man was leaning back, whistling softly between his teeth. He felt like telling Montano that he couldn't go through with it. He started to speak, then stopped, his blood icing over.

If I try to argue with him, I'll never get out of here alive. It means too much to him.

Do I just salve my conscience with that, then? Sit here and let them die?

With a shock of remembrance, it came to Bart that he had a weapon. He was armed. The energon-beam that was part of his uniform. Montano had evidently forgotten it. *Could* he kill Montano? Even to save two dozen Lhari?

He reached hesitantly towards the beam-gun; quickly thumbed the catch down to the lowest point, which was simple shock. He froze as Montano looked in his direction, hand out of sight under his cloak.

'How many Lhari on board?'

'Twenty-three, and three Mentorians.'

'Anyone apt to be behind shielding – say in the drives chamber?'

'No, I think they're all outside.'

Montano nodded, idly. 'Then we won't have to worry.'

Bart slipped his hand towards his weapon. Montano saw the movement, cocked his head in question; then, as understanding flashed over his face, his hand darted to his own gun, but Bart had pressed the charge of his, and Montano slumped over without a cry. He looked so limp that Bart gasped; was he dead? Hastily he fumbled the lax hand for a pulse. After a long, endless moment he saw Montano's crest twitch and he knew the man was breathing; shallow breaths.

Well, Montano would be safe here in the bunker. Hastily, Bart looked at his timepiece. Half an hour before the radiation was lethal – *for the Lhari*. Was it already, for him? Shakily, he unfastened the door. He ran out into the glare, seeing as he ran that his badge was tinged with an ever-darkening gold, orange... Montano had said there was a safety margin, but maybe he was wrong, maybe all Bart would accomplish would be his own death! He ran back along the line of bunkers, his heart pounding with his racing feet. Two crewmen came along the line, young white-crested Lhari from the other watch. He gasped, 'Where is the Captain?'

'Down that way – what's wrong, Bartol?' But Bart was gone, his muscles aching with the unaccustomed effort inside gravity; putting on speed as he saw the tall, austere shape of Vorongil, his banded cloak dark against the glaring light. Vorongil turned at the sound of his running feet.

'The crystal creatures have all gone away! Bartol – my dear young fellow, what's the matter?'

So much had happened to Bart in the last few minutes that it seemed he must have been gone for half a day; it was a shock to hear Vorongil say calmly, 'You're out of breath. Surely you're not finished already!'

'No, but unless you listen, you are!' Bart gasped.

Suddenly he realised that he was still holding his energon-beam gun. He dropped it and Vorongil stared, his eyes suddenly alert. 'What's this? What's happened?'

'Captain, go warn the men! They'll all be dead in half an hour! There are lethal radiations –' he started to hold up his badge, realised that the Lhari could not see colour and it would only be a darker spot against his clothing. Vorongil bent to pick up the fallen gun. 'Are you moonstruck?' he demanded, 'or mad? What's this

143

babble?'

'Captain Vorongil, they're going to kill everyone on the *Swiftwing* –'

'Speak Lhari!' Vorongil demanded, and Bart realised that in his excitement he had been babbling in Universal. He drew a long deep breath. 'Captain,' he said quietly, 'there are lethal radiations being released here. They want to capture the ship. You've just barely half an hour to warn the men, get them all inside – behind shielding.'

'What insane story is this?' Vorongil remained unruffled. 'How do you know? The radiation counter is out of order. How can you possibly know –'

Bart stood in despair. He had never envisaged the possibility that Vorongil might not even believe him. He felt like saying 'Check that bunker –' but even if Montano was a would-be murderer, he could not betray him to the Lhari. Well, he might as well go all the way! He heard his own voice rise hysterically.

'Captain, there's not *time!* I tell you, you'll all be dead if you don't listen! Gather the men! Get them into the ship! How can I get you to believe me? Captain, you don't know that I'm not a Lhari –'

'*What?*'

One of the Lhari crewmen came dashing up, his face pale and sweat-streaked. 'Captain, Rugel has collapsed! We can't figure out what's wrong with him!'

'It's the radiation,' Bart said desperately, and Vorongil reached out, catching Bart a cruel, taloned grip by the arm. Bart said desperately, 'I'm not a Lhari! I'm a Vegan! I signed on in disguise, I knew they meant to take the ship, but I couldn't let you all die – you don't believe me. Look –' abruptly, desperately, he reached up. 'Look at my eyes!' Pain stabbed through his eyes as he blinked and removed the dark contact lenses, holding them out to Vorongil. He could not see the Captain''s

144

face but suddenly two Lhari were holding him, and Vorongil was staring as if at some small, very dangerous reptile, his energon-gun in his hand. The fear of death was on him, but it no longer mattered. He saw through watering eyes the deepening orange of his radiation badge. 'Here,' he said, tearing at it, 'radiation. You must be able to see how dark it is. Even if it's just darkness. . . .'

Suddenly Vorongil was shouting, but Bart could not hear. Two men were dragging him along. They hustled him up the ramp of the ship. He could see again, but his eyes were blurred, and he felt sick, colours spinning before his eyes, a nauseated ringing in his head. At first he thought it was his ears ringing, then he made out the rising, the shrieking wail and fall of the emergency siren, steps running, shouting voices, the slow clang of the doors. Someone was pushing at him, babbling words in Lhari, but he heard them through an ever-increasing distance. Vorongil's face bent over his, only a blurred crimson blot that flashed away like a vanishing star in the viewport. It flamed out into green darkness, vanished, and Bart fell through what seemed to be a bottomless chasm of starless night.

When he woke, acceleration had its crushing hand on his chest. He tried to move, discovered that he was strapped hard into a bunk, and fainted again.

Suddenly the pressure was gone and he was lying at ease on the smooth sheets of a hospital bunk. His eyes were covered with a light bandage, and there was a sharp pain in his left arm; he tried to move it and found it was tied down.

'I think he's coming round,' said Vorongil's voice.

'Yes, and a lot too soon for me,' said a bitter voice which Bart recognized as that of the ship's Medic. 'Freak!'

145

'Listen, Baldy,' said Vorongil, 'whoever he is, he could have been blinded or killed. You wouldn't be alive now if it wasn't for that *freak*, as you call him. Bartol, can you hear me? Can you – how much light can your eyes stand?'

'As much as any Mentorian,' Bart said. He found he could move his right arm, and twitched the bandage away. Vorongil and the Medic stood over him; in the other infirmary bunk a form was lying covered with a white sheet. Sickly, Bart wondered if they had found Montano. Vorongil followed the direction of his eyes.

'Yes,' he said, and his voice held deep bitterness. 'Poor old Rugel is dead. He didn't get much of the radiation, but his heart wouldn't stand it, and gave out.' He bowed his head. 'He was bald in the service of the ships when my crest was new-sprouted,' he said in deep grief. 'He was an officer on my first ship.'

Bart felt the shock of that, even through his own fear. He looked down at his left arm. It was strapped to a splint, and fluid was dripping slowly into the vein there. Vorongil nodded. 'I expect you feel pretty sick,' he said. 'You got a good dose of radiation yourself, but we've given you a couple of transfusions – one of the Mentorians matched your blood type, fortunately. It was a close all.'

The Medic was looking down in ill-disguised curiosity. 'Fantastic,' he said. 'I don't suppose you'd tell me who changed your looks. I admit I wouldn't believe it until I had a look at your foot bones under the fluoroscope.'

Vorongil said quietly, 'Bartol – I don't suppose that's your real name – why did you do it?'

'I couldn't see you all die, sir,' Bart said, not expecting them to believe him. 'No more than that.'

The Medic said roughly in Lhari, 'It's a trick, sir, no more. A trick to make us trust him!'

146

'Why would he risk his own life then?' Vorongil asked. 'No, it's more than that.' He hesitated. 'We checked the bunkers – in radiation suits – before we took off. We found a man in one of them.'

'Did I – was he dead?' Bart whispered.

'No,' Vorongil said quietly.

'Thank God!' It was a heartfelt explosion. Then, apprehensively, 'Or – did you kill him?'

'What do you think we are?' Vorongil said incredulously. 'Bloodthirsty? Indeed no. His own men have probably found him by now. I don't imagine he got half as much radiation as you did.'

Bart surveyed the needle in his arm. 'Why are you taking all this trouble, if I'm going to be put out of the way?'

'You must have some funny ideas about us,' Vorongil said, shaking his head. 'That would be a fine way to reward you for saving all our lives. No, you're not going to be killed.'

'If I had my way –' the old Medic began, and suddenly Vorongil flew into a rage. 'This is my ship and I'm still in command! I'm tired of hearing about what you'd do to him! I'll decide what's to be done!'

'The laws of the High Council relating to Mentorians and other Second Galaxy citizens –'

'Oh, go quote laws to the exhaust pipes!' Vorongil said rudely. 'Get out!' The Medic went stiffly through the door, and Vorongil stood gazing down at Bart, slowly shaking his yellowed crest. 'I don't suppose I'll ever understand,' he said. 'I don't know what to say to you. It was a brave thing you did – but perhaps no braver than you've done all along. You – are you a Mentorian?'

'Only half.'

'I see. Your eyes. Odd,' he said, looking into space, 'that I could talk to you as I did by the monument there,

147

and you knew what I meant. But yes; you would understand. About bravery, and a leap into the unknown – yet I'd never have thought it possible of your race –' Abruptly he came to himself, and his voice was thin and cold.

'Well, I suppose that explains how you turned up, so luckily, just when we were short a man. I haven't quite decided what we're going to do with you. I haven't mentioned it to the crew yet,' he added, 'the fewer who hear this and spread it around, the better. Until I do decide – Bartol, I've told the crew that you got a heavy dose of radiation, and you're too sick to see visitors.' He sounded kinder when he said, 'It's true, you know. It won't hurt you to rest up and get your strength back.'

He went out, and Bart wondered, *get my strength back for what?* He lay back, feeling weaker than he realised. It was a relief to know he wasn't going to be killed out of hand, anyway. And somehow he didn't believe he was going to be killed or hurt at all. Vorongil had sounded too honestly shocked at the very idea.

It wasn't like being a prisoner. They brought him plenty of food and urged him to eat – 'You need plenty of protein after a radiation burn,' the Medic said. And if he stayed in his bunk, it was only because he felt too weak to get up. He did not realise it, but he was suffering from delayed emotional shock as well as from the radiation sickness. It wasn't any worse than the trip he'd made from Earth to Procyon Alpha; he'd been afraid then, too, and he hadn't known what was going to happen.

Inevitably, the time came when he had to think about what he had done. He had betrayed Montano and his people; he had been false to the conspiracy which had sent him.

But they don't know the Lhari, his conscience replied, justifying what he had done.

148

You sided with the Lhari against your own people.

Because my people were wrong and the Lhari were right. They didn't deserve to die. It wasn't war; it was treachery. Montano was planning cold-blooded murder, and I stopped it.

You spoilt our chance of learning about the Lhari fuel-catalyst, his invisible accuser charged him.

And the voice of his conscience replied:

I've done something better, better than simply stealing a secret by stealth. I've proved that humans and Lhari *can* trust each other, that they *can* communicate if they try. They can live together, and be friends. It's only their looks that are strange to one another. Ringg isn't any more alien than Tom. A kind, generous man is a kind generous man, whether his name is Raynor Three or Vorongil.

But who's going to know it? Demanded the voice of his despair, and his internal defender replied stoutly *I know it. And the truth comes out, sooner or later.* Somehow, a better understanding between men and Lhari will come of it.

Secure in this, he turned over and went peacefully to sleep.

When he woke again, he felt better. Rugel's body had been taken away from the other bunk, and the Mentorian girl Meta was sitting quietly at the cabinet between the bunks, watching him. He started to turn over, flinched at the pain in his arm.

'Yes,' she said, 'we're giving you one last transfusion. Plasma, this time. It's Lhari, but I suppose, if you know so much, you know that it won't hurt you.' She came and inspected the needles in his arm, and Bart caught her hand with his free one. 'Meta – does anyone else know?'

She looked down at him with a troubled smile, and shook her head. 'No,' she said. 'I was off watch a few hours ago, waiting for coldsleep – we're about to make

149

the long jump – when Vorongil came to my quarters, I was startled almost out of my wits; we Mentorians almost never see the Captain. He simply asked me if I could keep a secret, and then he told me about you. Oh, Bart!' It was a cry, and her small soft hand closed convulsively on his, 'I was so afraid! Afraid of what would happen when you were discovered! I knew they wouldn't kill you, but I was afraid –'

Yet they had killed David Briscoe, Bart thought, and hunted down two of his friends. It was the only thing he couldn't square with his perception of the Lhari. It didn't fit. He could understand that they had shot down the robocab with Edmund Briscoe in it, in pure self-defence, and that knowledge has taken off the edge of the horror. But the death of young Briscoe and everyone he had talked to could not be explained away.

'You seem very sure they wouldn't have killed me, Meta,' he said, carefully clasping his hand around hers.

'They wouldn't,' she affirmed. 'But they could – make you forget –'

A small chill went over Bart; he let go of her hand and lay staring bleakly at the wall. He supposed that was his probable fate; remembering the tragic tone of Raynor Three when he said *I won't remember you,* he gritted his teeth, feeling his face twist convulsively. Meta, watching, misunderstood.

'Arm hurting? I'll have that needle out of your arm in a few minutes now.'

When she had freed his arm and put away the apparatus, she came to his side. 'Bart, how did it happen? How did they find you out?'

Suddenly, the longing for human contact was too much for Bart, and the knowledge of his secret intolerable. The Lhari could find out what he knew, if they wanted to know, very simply; he was in their power. It didn't matter any more. 'I might as well start

150

at the beginning. Come and sit down by me, won't you? And let's talk Universal. I've been speaking Lhari until I've half forgotten I have my own language. I told you my name is Bart Steele. It all began three days after I graduated from the Space Academy on Earth, when I went to the Lhari spaceport to meet my father. . . .'

The telling of the story took a long time, and when he finished, Meta's soft small kitten-like face was compassionate.

'I'm glad you – did what you did,' she whispered. 'It's what a Mentorian would have done. I know that other races call us *Slaves of the Lhari*. We aren't. We're working in our own way to show the Lhari that human beings can be trusted. The other peoples – they hold away from the Lhari, fighting them with words even though they're afraid to fight them with weapons, carrying on the war that they're afraid to fight! Did it ever occur to you – all the peoples of all the planets keep saying, *we're as good as the Lhari*, but only the Mentorians are willing to prove it? The other people keep yelling about independence, and demanding that the Lhari *give* them the superdrive – and by that very demand they make the Lhari into supermen and gods! While the others yell for their rights, we're *working* for them! Bart, a Lhari ship can't get along in our galaxy without Mentorians any more. It may be slower than trying to take the warpdrive by force, or steal it by spying, but when we learn to endure it, I have faith that we'll get it!'

Bart, although moved by Meta's philosophy, couldn't quite share it. It still seemed to him that the Mentorians were lacking in something – independence, maybe, or drive.

'I wasn't thinking about anything like that,' he said honestly. 'It was simply that I couldn't let them die. After all –' he was speaking more to himself that to the girl, 'it's *their* stardrive. *They* found it. And they've given

151

us star trade and star travel, cheaply and with profit to both sides. Why should we dictate how they do it? When humans landed on a new country, before space, or on a new planet after it, well, we exploited it for our own profit as long as we could. I hope we'll get the stardrive some day. But if we got it by mass murder it would sow the seeds of hatred between men and Lhari that would never end. It wouldn't be worth it, Meta. Nothing would be worth that. We've got enough hate already.'

Bart was still in his bunk, but beginning to fret at staying there, when the familiar trembling of Acceleration Two, premonitory to the shift into warpdrive, started to run through the ship. It was, by now, so familiar to him that he hardly gave it a second thought, but Meta panicked.

'What's happening? Bart, what is it, why are we under acceleration again?'

'Shift to warp,' he said without thinking, and her face went deathly white. 'So that's it,' she whispered. 'Vorongil – no wonder he wasn't worried about what I would find out from you, or what you knew.' She drew herself together in her chair, a miserable shrunken terrified little figure, bravely trying to control her terror, then she held out her hands to Bart. 'I – I-m ashamed,' she whispered. 'When you've been so brave, I shouldn't be afraid to d-die –'

'Meta, what's the matter? What are you afraid of?'

'Can't you see?' she said almost hysterically, 'that's what he's going to do with us! Just shift into the warpdrive – not give us coldsleep, or drugs, just let us – die in the warpdrive –'

It suddenly swept over Bart what she meant, and what she feared. 'But don't you understand, Meta?' he exclaimed. 'What do you think the whole point of my disguise was? Humans *can* live through the warpdrive! No drugs, no coldsleep – Meta, I've done it dozens of times!'

'*But you're a Lhari!*' It burst from her, uncontrollable; she stopped, looked at him in consternation. He smiled, bitterly.

'No, Meta, they didn't do a thing to my internal organs, to my brain, to the tissues of my body! Just a little plastic surgery on my hands, my feet and my face,' he told her. 'Did you think *that* was why I lived through it? Meta, there's nothing to be afraid of – nothing,' he repeated.

She twisted her small hands together. 'I'm – trying to – believe that,' she whispered,'but all my life I've known –'

The screaming whine in the ship gripped them with the strange, clawing lassitude and discomfort; Bart, gasping under it, heard the girl moan, saw her slump lax in her chair, half fainting. Her face was so deathly white that he began seriously to be afraid she would die of fear. Fighting his own agonising weakness, he pulled himself upright; forcing his hands through the sluggishness of rising acceleration (outside the ship the star-trails began to lengthen as the warp frequencies flung them faster than light) Bart reached the girl, dug his claws cruelly into her.

'Girl, get hold of yourself! Fight it! *Fight* it! The more scared you are, the worse it's going to be!'

She was rigid, trembling, in a trance of terror.

'You rotten little coward,' he shouted at her, 'snap out of it! Or are all you Mentorians so soft, so gutless that you believe any half-baked folktale the Lhari pass off on you! You and your fine talk about earning the right to the stardrive! What would you do with it if you got it – if you die of fear when you try going through with it?'

'Oh! You – !' She flung back her head, her white face reddening with fury, her grey eyes blazing with rage. 'What do you think you are? Anything you can do, I can do too!' He saw life flowing back into her face, and her trembling now was with rage, not fear; she was fighting the pain, the crawling, burning itch in her nerve ends, the terrible sense of draining disorganization that came from the unbearable, shrieking strain in the fibres of the ship. Bart felt his own hold on himself breaking. He whispered hoarsely, 'That's the girl – don't be scared if I – black out for a minute –' he held on to consciousness with his last courage, afraid if he fainted, the girl would collapse again. 'Some people do....'

She reached for him, in the extremity of fear, and Bart, starved for some human touch, drew the girl into his arms. They clung together helplessly, like children; he felt her wet face against his own, the softness of her trembling hands. She was still crying a little. Then the blackness closed on him, as if endless, and the grey blur of warpdrive peak blotted his brain into nothingness.

He came out of it to feel her cheek soft against his, her head trustingly on his shoulder. He said huskily, 'All right, Meta?'

'I'm fine,' she murmured shakily. He tightened his hands a little, realising for the first time in months he had physically forgotten his Lhari disguise, that Meta had given him this priceless reassurance that he was human. But, as if suddenly aware of it again, she looked up at him and drew hesitantly away.

'Don't – Meta, am I so horrible to you, then? So – repulsive?'

'No, it's only –' she bit her lip. 'It's just that the Lhari are – can't quite explain it.'

'Different,' Bart finished for her. 'If you'd looked at your own face in the mirror that way for months – at first it was horrible. I was repelled – physically repelled by myself, and by them. It was like living among weird animals, and being one of the animals. And then, one day, Ringg was just another kid. He had grey skin and long claws and white hair, just the way I had pinkish skin and short fingernails and reddish hair, but the difference wasn't that I was human inside and he wasn't. If you skinned Ringg, and skinned me, we'd be almost identical. Oh, a few little bones in the feet and fingers, the cartilage in our noses and ears, yes; but an Aldebaranian and I are just as different as that. And this much light would have blinded my own father. And all of a sudden then, Ringg and Vorongil and all the rest were men to me. Just people. I thought you Mentorians, after living with the Lhari all these years, would feel that.'

She said in slow wonder, 'We've lived and worked side by side with them all these years, yet kept so apart! I've defended the Lhari to you, yet it took you to explain them to me!'

His arm was still around her, her head still laying on his shoulder. Bart was just beginning to wonder if he might kiss her when the infirmary door opened and Ringg stood in the doorway, staring at them with surprise, shock, and revulsion. Bart realised, suddenly, how it must look to Ringg – who certainly shared Meta's prejudice – but even as he comprehended it, Ringg's face altered. Meta slipped from Bart's arms and rose, but Ringg came slowly into the room.

'I remembered you had a bad reaction to warpdrive,' he said, 'I came to see if you were all right. I would never have believed – but I'm beginning to guess. There was always something about you, Bartol.' He shut the door behind him and stood against it. His voice lowered almost to a whisper, he said, 'You're not Lhari, are you?'

'Vorongil knows –' Bart said.

Ringg nodded. 'That day on Lharillis. The crew was talking, but only one or two of them really *know* what happened. There are a dozen rumours. I wanted to see you. They said you were sick with radiation burns –'

'I was.'

'But you're not now, are you?' He raised his hand slowly to the claw marks on his forearm; saw Bart watching him and smiled.

'You're not worrying about that fight, are you? Forget it, friend. If anything, I admire someone who can use his claws – especially if, as I begin to suspect, they aren't his.' He leaned over, his hand lightly on Bart's shoulder. 'I don't forget so easy,' he said. 'You saved my life, remember? And you're a hero on the ship for warning us all. Are you really human? Why not get rid of the disguise? By now it wouldn't make any difference what you were!'

Bart laughed wryly. 'It won't come off,' he said, and explained. Ringg raised his hands to his own face curiously. 'I wonder what sort of looking human I'd make?' He turned his hands over; bent to look curiously at Meta's small fingers. 'Not that I'd ever have the nerve. But then, it's no surprise to anyone that you have courage, Bartol.'

'You – accept it?' Meta said, almost in a whisper.

'It's a shock,' Ringg said honestly. 'It scares me a little. But I'm remembering the friendship. That was real. We got along, we were friends. Why shouldn't we be now?'

Bart felt warmed and reassured. But as he looked from Ringg to Meta, he realised none of this would mean anything until he knew what Vorongil would do – and what was going to happen to him.

Chapter Eleven

Captain Vorongil did not leave him long in suspense.
He had hardly got over the shock, and Ringg was still
bending over Meta's hand, when the captain came
unexpectedly into the room. He started to speak, then
noticed Ringg.

'I might have known,' he said. 'If there was anything
to find out, you'd find it out.'

'Shall I go, *rieko mori*?'

'No, stay,' growled Vorongil, 'you'll find it out
anyhow, some way or other, you might as well get it
right the first time. Just keep yourself from gossiping
about it, if you can. But first of all – are you all right,
Meta?' he asked the Mentorian.

She nodded, rising to her feet. Her chin went up,
almost defiantly. 'Why! Why have you lied to us all this
time?'

Vorongil looked mildly startled. 'Well, well, it wasn't
a lie,' he said, not unkindly. 'Nine out of ten Lhari
captains believe it with all their heart – that humans will
die in warpdrive. I wasn't sure myself, until I heard the
debates in Council City last year. I'd never have tried
the experiment if I hadn't had you on board, Bartol.'

'But why?' Bart added his question to Meta's, and
Vorongil sighed. His eyes, grey and keen, rested
disconcertingly on Bart's. 'I presume you know human
history,' he said, 'better than I do. The Lhari have never

157

had a war. Quite frankly, you terrified us. To give ourselves a breathing time, it was decided on the highest summit levels that we wouldn't give humans too many chances to find out things we preferred to keep to ourselves. The first few ships to carry Mentorians carried them without drugs or coldsleep, but then the policy went into effect of having them drugged, and people forget easily. The truth is buried in the records of those early voyages. As the Mentorians grew more important to us, we began to regret the policy – but by then our temporary device had got out of hand. The Mentorians themselves believed it so firmly that when we tried the experiment of carrying them through the shift into warpdrive they died of fear. I tried it with you, Meta, because I knew that Bart's very presence would reassure you. The others were given an inert sedative they believed to be the coldsleep drug. They're fine. I'll let you tell them. How are you feeling now, Bart?'

'Fine – but wondering what's going to happen.'

'You won't be hurt,' Vorongil said quickly. Then, 'You don't believe me, do you?'

'I don't, sir. David Briscoe did what I did – and he's dead. So are three other men.'

Vorongil sat down. He sighed. 'Men do strange things from fear – men and Lhari. Your people, as I said before, have a strange history. It scares us. If you knew the coordinates of the Lhari stars – can you guarantee that some, at least, of your people wouldn't try to come and take the secret of stardrive by force? We left a man on Lharillis who would have killed 24 of us for that chance. I suppose the captain of the *Multiphase*, knowing he had gravely violated Lhari law, knowing that if Briscoe's report spread too far it might touch off an intergalactic war between men and Lhari – I suppose he felt that half a dozen deaths were better than half a million. I'm not defending him. Just, maybe, explaining.'

Bart lowered his eyes. He had no answer to that.

'But about you,' Vorongil said. 'No, you won't be killed. But that's all I can guarantee. My personal feelings have nothing to do with the matter. You'll have to go to Lharis with us, and you'll have to be psych-checked there by the High Council to see if you know anything that's dangerous to us. That is a Lhari law – and, by treaty with your Federation, it's a human law, too. And if you know anything dangerous to us, we have a legal right to eliminate those memories before you can be released in your home world again.'

Meta smiled at him, but Bart shivered. That was almost worse than the thought of death.

The thought grew more oppressive as the ship forged on through the system of the home world of the Lhari, where their last jump had taken them. He had nightmares of Raynor Three, and though Meta and Ringg visited him almost every watch and tried to keep him cheered up, he felt a nervous wish to have all the talking over with.

Almost the worst of it was the fear that he might forget Meta. The pretty Mentorian girl had become a symbol to him now, and he had lost so many of his friends. But when he spoke of his fear one day, she reassured him.

'You don't exactly forget,' she said. 'You just have a block against – well, for instance, I *know* the coordinates of the fuelling stop. But I couldn't reveal them, even under deep hypnosis or narcosynthesis. They tell me that, after years and years, this *does* begin to affect the memory. And the coldsleep drug affects the memory, too. Eventually, most Mentorians begin to be affected by it.'

'But Raynor Three –' Bart stopped. Raynor Three had been *doubling* the Lhari game. The Lharis had made him unable to tell humans what he knew of their secrets – *and humans had, by his own choice, made him unable to tell the*

159

Lhari what he knew of the conspiracy against the Lhari. He had chosen to erase all his memories, human techniques of mental blocking being inferior.

Nevertheless, he feared it, and his fear did not grow less when, after the ordeal of planetary deceleration, they touched down and he was taken off the ship under guard, with only a glimpse, through dark glasses, at the terrible brilliance of the pure-white Lhari sun dazzling on crystal towers, before he was hustled into a closed surface vehicle.

It whisked him away to a building he did not see from the outside; he was taken by a private lift to a suite of rooms which might, for all the clues he could get from their contents, have been a suite in a luxury hotel, a jail, or a lunatic asylum. The walls were translucent; the furniture oddly coloured, and so carefully padded that even a homicidal or suicidal person could not have hurt himself or anyone with it or on it. Food – strange, and unidentifiable – reached him often enough so that he never got hungry, but not often enough to keep him from being bored between meals, or from brooding. Two enormous Lhari came in to look at him every hour or so, but either they were deaf and dumb, did not understand his dialect of Lhari, or were under orders not to speak to him or answer his questions. It was the most frustrating time of his entire voyage, and after what he imagined was four days, he began to be terrified. Maybe they simply intended to shut him up here, in safe obscure confinement, for the rest of his life! Maybe that was what Vorongil meant when he had said, *You won't be harmed.*

Abruptly, it ended. A Lhari, and a Mentorian interpreter who spoke not only Universal, but Bart's own Vegan home language, came for him, and took him down elevators and up stairs into a quiet neutral room where four Lhari were gathered. They sat him in a comfortable chair and the Mentorian interpreter said gently, with apology:

'Bart Steele, I have been asked to say to you that you will not be physically harmed in any way. This will be much simpler, and will have much less injurious effect on your mind, if you cooperate with us. At the same time, I have been asked to remind you that resistance is absolutely useless, and if you attempt it, you will only be treated with force rather than with courtesy.'

Bart sat facing them, shaking with humiliation. The thought of resistance flashed through his mind. Maybe he should make them fight for what they got! They'd get it anyway, but by God, he didn't have to sit here submissively and hand it to them on a platter, did he? At least they'd see that all humans weren't like the Mentorians, to sit quietly and let themselves be brainwashed without a word of protest – he started to spring up, and the hands of his guards tightened, swift and strong, even before his muscles had fully tightened. Bart's head dropped. Cold common sense doused over his brave thoughts. He was uncountable millions of light-years from his own people. He was absolutely alone. Bravery would mean nothing; submission would mean nothing. Would he be more of a man, somehow, if he let his mind be wrecked? What he knew, he was somehow sure, they had a good idea of already.

'All right,' he muttered, 'I won't fight.'

'You show your good sense,' the Mentorian said quietly. 'Give us your left arm, please – or if you are left-handed, your right. As you prefer.'

He was giving in. It was the low point of his life.

He felt a needle slide in under the skin of his left arm. A dizzying welter of thoughts spun through his mind. Briscoe. Raynor One and Raynor Three. The net between the stars. Ringg, Vorongil, Meta... his father....

Consciousness slid away.

The Mentorian was holding a cup to his lips. He swallowed, coughed and realised, as his head cleared, that he had been given some strong stimulant. He was alone in a quiet room with the Mentorian assistant, who said courteously, 'When you feel able, the High Council are waiting for you. A transcript of your questions and answers will be made available to you afterwards if you wish.'

Bart blinked, surprised at how clear his mind felt. As if exploring a sore tooth with the tongue, his mind sought for memories, but he still felt the humiliation and resentment against the Lhari, the details clear and uncomplicated of his voyage here. Montano's conspiracy, everything he had done or said. They could easily have changed my attitudes... and they didn't. They could have made me loyal to the Lhari, and they didn't. I'm the same as I was before.

'I'm ready now,' he said, puzzled, and followed the Mentorian along a corridor. The Mentorian pushed at a door, said softly, 'The Vegan, Bart Steele, alias Bartol,' in Lhari, and Bart stepped into a large, imposing room.

He faced a low, semicircular barricade of glassy non-coloured metal behind which eight Lhari, old, and as bald as so many eggs, sat facing him. Their eyes rested on him with frank curiosity; one smiled, another frowned, one said 'Surprising!' and a fourth turned slightly:

'Captain Vorongil, do you identify this man?'

'I do,' Vorongil said. In the bright lights of the room Bart had not seen him sitting before the eight Lhari, whom he took to be the High Council.

'Come here, Bart Steele, alias Bartol,' said the ancient Lhari at the centre of the semi-circle.

Slowly Bart walked forward. Before their wise eyes he felt suddenly very young, very frightened – and very foolish.

Here he'd been thinking of himself as a brave spy, a gallant conspirator, a fighter in humanity's cause and what not, and before their knowing, wise, ancient eyes, their gnomish lined faces, he saw himself as what he was: a reckless boy, playing with intrusive schemes to meddle in other people's affairs. He lowered his eyes before them.

The old Lhari said calmly, 'We have read the transcript of your knowledge. There is very little that we do not know in it. We are not, of course, concerned with human plots and conspiracies unless they endanger Lhari lives, but the Antares authorities, under treaty, will deal with the man Montano for an unauthorised landing on Lharillis and a violation of the Intergalactic Treaty.' He smiled suddenly and said, 'Bartol, or whatever you call yourself, you are a brave young man. I suppose you are afraid we will block your memories of what has happened, or your ability to speak of them?'

Bart nodded, gulping. Was the old Lhari able to read his thoughts?

'A year ago, we might have done so. Captain Vorongil – you will be interested to know that we have discussed this in Council, and your recommendations have been taken. The secret that humans can endure warpdrive has outlived its usefulness. For good or ill, it is no longer secret. We cannot possibly eliminate all the old records, or the enterprising young people who hunt them out. The captain who had David Briscoe killed is undergoing psychotherapy and will soon recover, we hope, from the horrible trauma of having killed an intelligent being. As for the rest –' he spread his hands in a surprisingly human gesture. 'Bart Steele, you know nothing that is a danger to us. You do not know the coordinates of our world here. You do not know the location of our fuelling stop. You know nothing that is not common knowledge, or soon to become common knowledge. We have decided not to interfere with your memories or your ability to verbalise them. Talk as much as you like. And may the memory of this voyage help relations between Lhari and other human races than the Mentorians. Good luck to you,' he added, and he was smiling.

Another of the ancients, seated beside him, spoke before Bart could react. 'There is another side to this. You have broken a treaty between Lhari and man. We have dealt with you; now your own people must do so. We have decided not to press charges; it may be that they will be equally lenient. But you must be taken back, on the *Swiftwing*, to the planet where the violation originated. There, you and the man Raynor Three will face charges of unlawful conspiracy to board a Lhari ship in violation of the Intergalactic Trade Act. Captain Vorongil, will you be responsible for him?'

So it's not over yet, Bart thought drearily. *I've lost. I didn't even learn anything important enough for them to want to suppress it.* There was a strange, wounded pride in this; after all his trouble, he was being treated like a little boy who has used a great deal of enterprise and bravery to rob a cookie cupboard, and for his pains is sent home with the stolen cookie in his hand, to a chorus of kindly laughter!

But Raynor Three! What will they do to him?

Vorongil touched his arm and said gently, 'Come with me, Bartol. I'm taking you back to the *Swiftwing*. I don't have to treat you like a prisoner, do I?'

Numbly Bart gave him what the old Lhari asked; his word of honour not to attempt to escape – *escape? Where to?* – or to enter the drives chamber of the *Swiftwing* while they were still in the Lhari worlds. 'It's for your own safety,' Vorongil told him kindly.

'It doesn't matter,' he said, and covered his face with his hands.

... with his *hands!*

He gasped, spread them before his face. He raised them again in amazement. They were a pale, suntanned-flesh colour. The fingers looked longer and thinner than he remembered them, but they were his own hands again. In amazement and shock, he felt of his ears, his nose, the very short, crisp hair growing on his newly-shaven skull.

'You fools!' said Vorongil to the Mentorian in disgust. 'Why didn't you tell him what the Medics had done for him? Easy, Bartol!' The old Lhari's arm was around his shoulder. 'I thought they'd told you. Someone come here and give the youngster a hand!'

Later, in the mirror of the small cabin – it had been Rugel's – which was to be his prison on the *Swiftwing*, he had a chance to study his strange-familiar face. He had supposed that only a few moments had elapsed between the moment the Lhari Medics had given him a shot and the time he awoke under stimulants. Actually it had been nearly two weeks during which time he had been kept under drugs for his face to heal.

As Raynor Three had warned, the change had not been wholly reversible. There was still a hint of something thin, strange, and alien in the set of his features; his hands would always be inhumanly long, thin, and supple. For the rest – he thought he looked older, his face somehow more set and hardened.

The first two weeks of the return voyage of the *Swiftwing* were a nightmare of frustration and boredom. Ringg came to see him now and then, trying to cheer him up, but he sensed that Ringg didn't quite know what to make of him. He felt cut off from Ringg, no longer a Lhari, and yet not quite human, either. Dimly, he thought, *I've come a long way, in more than one respect. I've got a long way back.*

He asked Ringg, once, 'I see you decided to sign out again. Did your family get used to the idea?'

Ringg shook his head. 'No,' he said, 'but I figured it like this. I'm older than you are. If you could do what you did, on your own, I'm old enough to do what I want to do, without worrying my family about it. I'm sorry if they don't like it. But I'm the one who's got to live it.'

They had been in space about fifteen days, and had made two warpdrive jumps from the Lhari world, when Vorongil came into his cabin one day.

'We're landing this afternoon on the last planet we will touch before leaving the First Galaxy,' the captain said. 'You had no chance to visit Lharis, Bartol... at least, not to see anything while you were there. The next jump will take us back into your galaxy. You came a long way for this; do you want to go ashore at the next stop?'

Bart asked, 'You think you can trust me?'

He felt that his bitterness was childish when Vorongil replied gravely, 'You don't know the coordinates of Lharis; you don't know the coordinates of this world, and you have no way of finding them. I don't want to coax or persuade you, but if it would give you any pleasure to visit the city, with Ringg and Meta, you have my permission.'

Behind the formal words, Bart sensed a reluctance at making a prisoner of him; a wish to be kind; even, perhaps, that the old Lhari understood his sense of defeat. Nothing was to be gained by sulking in his cabin.

He had been aboard ship so long, or so it seemed, that the air seemed strange when he came out into the brilliant light of the Lhari spaceport. He was wearing Lhari clothing – he had no others – and he supposed that he would pass for a Mentorian. *His mother must have been under the strange sun of this world.* What colour was the star? At first he had thought it a pure white sun, yet now it seemed more like a red, now like a blue – *this is crazy; is it purple?* He turned to Meta, finally, irritated by his inability to decide.

'Meta, what colour is this sun? I've been all around the spectrum and I can't make up my mind! It's not red, blue, green, orange, violet, or all of them at once, but –'

He stopped, abruptly realising what he had said and what he had seen. 'It's an eighth colour –' he finished, almost anti-climactically.

'You and your talk of colours,' Ringg grumbled, 'I wish I knew what you Mentorians *see!*' He shook his head in disgust. 'It's like trying to imagine seeing a smell or a sound, or hearing light!'

Meta's light laughter made him smile sheepishly. She said to Bart, 'As far as I know, no one's ever named it. The Mentorians call it "catalyst colour", sometimes. I think only Mentorians' eyes, or those with eyes like ours, can see it as a separate colour. Once, during a landing, some passengers from Earth and Capella saw the fuel catalyst – the Lhari aren't particularly concerned to keep it out of sight – and to them it looked colourless.'

A wild excitement was gusting up in Bart. He acquiesced to Ringg's suggestion that they take a skycab and tour the port, but he hardly saw the tall pylons, the sweeping roads and low many-coloured cities scattered around the spaceport. His thoughts were racing. *There can't be too many suns this colour*, he thought. And telescopes can reach the Lhari Galaxy from ours. Could success be salvaged from defeat? Maybe he need not go so empty-handed as he had thought from the Lhari worlds! They had dismissed him scornfully, stolen cookie in hand – but would it be a bigger cookie than they thought?

When I get home, he thought, I'll study starmaps, and analyse them, and find it that way. . . .

The exhilaration lasted almost an hour before he came, figuratively, down to earth. To pick one star, out of trillions – and not even one in his own galaxy? It would take a lifetime – and he wasn't even quite certain which of the four or five spiral nebulae *was* the Lhari

167

Galaxy. After they left Antares, they had made a warpdrive jump – but the faster-than-light drive did not take place through normal space; he could not even assume it was the nearest galaxy, in point of direction, from the rim of his own. By colour alone, without even a spectrographic analysis, to pick one star out of the whole universe? He didn't know the magnitude of the star, its size or its position. A lifetime? A *hundred* lifetimes wouldn't do it! The chances were one in about forty BILLION.

It had been a nice try, but it hadn't worked. He might have known that Vorongil wouldn't have taken the chance of letting him land on any Lhari world where he might conceivably have a chance of working out the position! Certainly not the star where – he guessed from the colour – they found, in its system, the curiously-coloured element which was their fuel.

After blastoff he visited the lounge with Ringg, and stood looking at the unfamiliar galaxy of the Lhari stars; the unknown, forever unknowable constellations, the strangely-coloured sun winking with strange familiarity as they left it behind. Where had he seen that colour? In his glimpse of the Lhari ship landing, so long ago on Earth? Of all the colours of space, this one he would never know. He turned away from the bewildering constellations and went to his cabin, to dream of the green star Meristem where he had first plotted known coordinates for a previously unknown world.

One more warpdrive shift, and Vorongil came again to his cabin, this time crisp and businesslike.

'We're back in your own galaxy,' he said, 'among the stars you know. We have no passenger space on the *Swiftwing*, Bartol, we had to ship out without replacing Rugel, and we didn't replace you. We're short two hands. I haven't any authority to ask this, but would you like your old job back for the rest of the voyage?'

He glanced at his human hands; Vorongil raised his yellowing crest and chuckled. 'It won't be the first time we've had Mentorians who knew as much about astrogation as the rest of the crew!'

Bart looked the old Lhari straight in the eye. He said: 'I won't accept Mentorian terms, Vorongil.'

'I wouldn't ask it,' Vorongil said. 'You worked your way out on this same run. The High Council didn't see fit to erase that knowledge from your mind. Why should I ask for it? Do you want to – or not?'

Did he want to! Not until this moment, buried in defeat, had Bart identified what the worst of his pain was; on the way out, he had been part of the ship. On the way back he was a passenger, a supercargo! Literally he ached to be back with it again! 'I do, Honourable Bald One,' he said, and Vorongil said, 'Very well. You go on duty at the next watch,' turned and walked out. His tone was sharp, no longer gently indulgent as it had been, and Bart, at first surprised, suddenly caught the difference.

He was no longer a prisoner, a passenger! Vorongil was his captain again – and he was part of the crew!

The crew of the *Swiftwing* were oddly constrained with him, at first, treating him as they did the Mentorians, but Ringg's friendly acceptance soon won almost the old footing. He had the freedom of the ship again, and with every watch it seemed he was building a bridge. He had been accepted among them as a Lhari. Now they were accepting him as a human....

But for what? He would never sign on an interstellar ship again. Something might come of it in the long run, but it would be too long for him. Jump followed jump, as the *Swiftwing* worked her way, taking on strange cargo and discharging it, from star to star. Antares, Aldebaran. And, at last, Procyon Alpha neared in the viewport. A year ago, frightened, unused to his disguise, terrified

169

among strange monsters, one of them himself, he had heard an unknown companion – *poor old Rugel, poor old Baldy* – ask which of the planets was Alpha, and had to keep from saying *the blue one*.

Meta came quietly into the lounge behind him. The Mentorians had their own recreation quarters, but no regulation prevented their coming here, and on this trip, at Ringg's encouragement, Meta and Bart had often joined him here. A sort of informal friendliness, never known between Lhari and Mentorian, had grown up among the three of them. It was small comfort, but such as it was, it helped a little to know that much good had come of his work.

'Bart –' Meta said softly.

He turned to face her. Most of the officers were on watch, or sleeping; they had the lounge to themselves.

'Well, it won't be much longer, Meta. Tomorrow we touch down on Alpha. And I'll find out what the Intergalactic Trade Treaty is going to do to me. *Conspiracy unlawfully to board a Lhari ship in violation –*' he repeated the charge dryly, with irony. 'At least, at very least, they'll send me home to Vega – and I'll spend the rest of my life managing business affairs!'

'It doesn't have to be that way,' Meta said.

'What other choice is there?'

'You're – half Mentorian,' she said, and caught his hand. 'Oh, Bart, you love it so! I know you can't bear to give it up – I never could! Stay with us! Please stay with us!'

Before answering, he looked out of the viewport a last time. The coloured clouds of cosmic dust swirled and foamed around the familiar jewel-stars of his own sky; blue Vega, the topaz sunburst of Sol where he had learned astrogation, Procyon where he had become a Lhari, the ruby of Aldebaran (hail and farewell, David Briscoe!), the crimson eye of Antares, where he had learned fear and his own integrity. The colours, the unknowable colours of space! And others. The blinding colour of a captive sun. The green star where he had plotted, unaided, his first warpdrive shift (how he had sweated over those coordinates! Even now they were burned indelibly on his mind!) and explored a cave of odd minerals, and broken his wrist dragging Ringg through a hailstorm to shelter, and where Meta had first seen through his disguise. Colour, again, yet a simple *black and blue* had given him away. He took a last, long, hungry look at the colours of space, then turned his back on them, deliberately giving them up. He could not pay the price the Mentorians paid.

'No, Meta – no, dear,' he said huskily, 'the Mentorian way is fine, and I'm not blaming them. But I had a taste of being one of the masters of space. It's more than most men ever have; maybe it's more than I deserve. But I'll never settle for anything less. Not even if it means losing you.' He shut his eyes and stood that way, head bowed. When he looked up again, he was alone in the lounge.

Chapter Twelve

The low rainbow building of Eight Colours, near the spaceport of Procyon Alpha, had not changed, and when Bart went in, as he had done a year ago, it seemed that the same varnished girl was sitting before the same glass desk, neon-edged and brittle, with the same chrome-tinged hair and blue fingernails. She looked at Bart in his Lhari clothing, at Meta in her Mentorian robe and cloak, at Ringg, and in her unruffled dignity did not turn a hair.

'May I help you?' she inquired, still not caring.

'I want to see Raynor One.'

'On what business, please?'

'Tell him,' said Bart, with immense satisfaction, 'that his boss is here – Bart Steele – and wants to see him right away.'

It had a sort of disrupting effect. She seemed to go blurred at the edges. After a minute, blinking carefully, she spoke into the visionscreen, and reported, numbly, 'Go on up, Mr. Steele.'

He wasn't expecting a welcome. He said so to Meta as the elevator rose. 'After all, if I'd never come back, he'd doubtless have inherited the whole Eight Colours line, unencumbered. I don't expect he'll be happy to see me. But if I have to face the Human-Lhari Intergalactic Trade Bureau, I need someone who can find counsel for

172

me. And Raynor One is the only one I can turn to.'

Vorongil - in whose custody he was - had accepted his parole to appear when he was summoned. Bart had no intention of trying to escape.

The elevator slid to a stop and opened. They stepped out; a man, walking nervously towards them, stopped and raised his head. For a moment, expecting to see Raynor One, Bart was deceived, then, as the man's face broke into a spreading smile of welcome, he stopped in incredulous delight.

'Raynor Three!'

The man gripped Bart by the shoulders in a hard grasp of welcome; in an overflowing gladness Bart hugged him. It was like meeting with the dead. He felt as if he had really come home.

'But, but - you remember me!' he exclaimed, stepping away and looking at Raynor Three in amazement. Slowly, the man nodded. His eyes were grave. 'Yes,' he said. 'I stayed here - didn't sign on again. I decided it wasn't worth it, Bart - to go on forgetting everything that meant anything to me. Even if it meant giving up space, and never travelling again except as a passenger. I wasn't going to go on being afraid to remember what I had done before, never knowing the consequences or responsibilities of my acts. That was a fool's paradise - and I didn't want it. What I've done, I've done.' He smiled his strangely beautiful smile, and said, 'The *Multiphase* sailed without me. I've been here - hoping some day I'd know the rest.'

Associations clicked into place in Bart's mind. The *Multiphase*. Raynor Three, then, was the Mentorian who had smuggled David Briscoe off the ship where he had stowed away - and whose memories, wrung out by the Lhari captain of that ship, had touched off the manhunt and many deaths. But Raynor Three had paid for all that! Glad as he was to see him, he was almost sorry. Raynor Three would have to face the charges with him. . . .

Raynor One got up from behind his desk and strode towards them. He looked sharply at Bart and said, 'So it is really you. I thought it might be another trap. You've changed – grown up. Word came from Antares that Montano had been caught on Lharillis, and his ship confiscated for an illegal landing. I thought you were surely dead.'

'We sent a boy to do a man's job,' Raynor Three said, 'and he came back a man.' He drew Bart along into the office, looking curiously at Ringg and Meta. 'But tell me – how did you get back your – your own face? Can I –'

'We can talk, yes,' Bart said. 'Ringg is my friend, and knows the whole story. Actually I came for help. I've got to face charges before the Human-Lhari Trade Bureau, and I'm afraid you do too.'

Raynor One burst out harshly, 'A trap after all, Three! He trapped you, and he's in league with the Lhari to lead them to you –'

'No,' Raynor Three said, 'or he wouldn't be walking around free and unguarded and with all his memories intact. Tell me about it, Bart.' And when Bart had given a quick narration of the Lhari judgment, he nodded slowly.

'That's all we ever wanted. Don't think you failed, Bart. The horrible part was only the way they were trying to keep it secret.' His face twisted into a convulsive spasm. 'Men from the *Multiphase*, hunting Briscoe down, tracking and killing the men he talked to, in secret –'

Ringg interrupted, 'Do not judge the Lhari by them, Raynor Three,' and Raynor Three said in good Lhari, 'I don't, feathertop. I know the Lhari, remember? Raynors have been working with the Lhari since the days of Rhazon of Nedrus. But I wanted an open, official

174

statement of Lhari policy; not secret murders by fanatics. I had confidence in the Lhari as a people, but not in individuals. What good did it do me – to know that the Lhari council in another galaxy would have condemned the murders and manhunts when they were going on day after day? Don't you see, Bart?' he continued. 'You didn't fail – not if we're going to have the publicity of a test case publicly heard. That means the Lhari are prepared to admit, before our whole galaxy, that men, that humans *can* survive warpdrive without coldsleep. That's all David Briscoe was trying to prove, or your father either – may they rest in peace. So, whatever happens, we've won.'

'If you two idealists will give me a minute for cold realities,' Raynor One said, 'there's this. Bart will need counsel. Among other things, he's not yet of legal age. The fact that he acted as he did, with the consent of his legal guardians, throws the responsibility on us – yes,' he added to Bart, 'your father appointed me your guardian. When I turned you over to Three, I'm afraid, I assumed responsibility. So I'll have to be responsible for your defence.'

'But I don't need a defence,' Bart said quietly. 'I'm going to tell the truth and let it stand.' He and Raynor Three exchanged nods of complete understanding.

Raynor One threw up his hands. 'You're both crazy,' he said. 'I give up!'

Bart walked around in front of the stern-faced Raynor One and grinned at him. 'Look,' he said softly, smiling past Raynor at Ringg, 'if I can cross two galaxies under my own steam, nobody's going to hold you responsible for my actions. You've got all the forethought and common sense in the family, maybe. But nobody will blame you if I don't let you hold my hand.'

'It'll be needed when you and Three go to the prison planets,' Raynor One said sourly, 'somebody will have to manage your affairs.'

'Well, then, I can leave 'em in good hands,' Bart said. Raynor One sighed and shook his head. 'When it gets around, I'll have another load off my mind,' he said. 'Some lunatic from Capella arrived here a couple of months ago, and all but accused me of having you murdered! Do you know a Tom Kendron? He's been haunting the place –'

Tom! Bart stopped him in mid-word with a demand for Tom's address, and an hour later they were all gathered by skycab at Raynor Three's country house, all talking at once far into the night. The Raynors both wanted to know every detail of Bart's experience, and Tom wanted to know everything. Bart himself, during the merry reunion, tried to forget that the next day might bring reprimand, imprisonment, delay indefinitely the day when he took up the burden his father had left of running Vega Interplanet and Eight Colours. The Lhari Council had told him to talk as much as he liked about his voyage, and when he repeated their words, 'It is our hope that from this voyage may come a better understanding of man and Lhari,' Tom leaned forward and seized his hands, gripping them tightly.

'You make them sound like pretty decent people,' he said, and looked at Ringg.

'A year ago, if you'd told me I'd be sitting down with a Lhari spaceman and a batch of Mentorians, I'd have laughed,' he said.

'And I, too, if one had said I would be beneath a human roof,' Ringg replied. 'But a friend to Bart is my friend.' He touched the faint, almost-invisble scars on his forehead, saying softly, 'But for Bart, I would not be here to greet anyone, Lhari or Mentorian, as friend.'

'So,' said Tom triumphantly, 'even if you didn't discover the secret of the eight colours, Bart, you've done part of what your father died for –'

Sudden light burst over Bart as he spoke. Once again he was in a cave under a green star, where Ringg lay unconscious and bleeding, and with his Lhari light playing over a waterfall of coloured minerals. *And there was one whose colour he could not identify . . . was it red, violet, blue, green, orange . . .* or under this Lhari light, some strange colour . . . never before seen elsewhere save in the shimmer of a landing Lhari ship, the colour of an unknown sun containing an unknown element, the colour of an unknown Lhari fuel. . . .

'Say that again,' he said abruptly.

'You've done part of what your father –'

'No. The part about the secret of the eight colours. Raynor, I'm an idiot!' he said, and stood up, his hands literally shaking in his excitement. 'No, don't ask me any questions. I could still be wrong. But even if it means a prison planet, it's not going to be a secret any more.'

Ringg had to go back to the ship that night; soon after he left, Raynor Three received an official notice, amounting to a subpoena, to appear before the Human-Lhari Trade Bureau the next day. The formal charges against them were conspiracy unlawfully to board a Lhari ship with intent to violate the Trade treaties thereto pertaining. He handed it to Bart.

'You weren't serious about not wanting a defence, Bart?'

'I was,' Bart said. 'All I want is a chance to tell my story in my own way. I don't believe our own people will be harder on me than the Lhari were. But even if they are, I want to tell it where everyone will hear me.'

Raynor Three looked at him curiously. 'There's something you're not telling, Bart.'

'There is.'

'Want to tell me?'

Bart hesitated, then shook his head. As nearly as possible, Raynor Three had stepped into his father's

177

place. It was possible that Raynor Three would approve his plan. He longed to share the burden. But Raynor Three had his own trouble, his own long burden of responsibility. He could not burden him with this, too. Raynor Three saw his hesitation and smiled, turning away.

'All right, son. Sorry I asked. You don't need to have the shocks cushioned any more.'

It was good to sleep under a human roof, in a soft human bed, good to get up and eat breakfast and shave and dress in ordinary human-style clothes again. But Bart folded his Lhari tights and cloak tenderly, with regret. They were the memory of an experience no one else would ever share. Raynor Three let him take the controls of the skycab as they flew back to the spaceport city, and a little before noon they entered the hallway of the great pylon of crystal and stone that was the headquarters of the Human-Lhari Trade Bureau on Procyon Alpha. Men and Lhari were moving in the crowds, the Lhari accompanied by Mentorian interpreters, and among them Bart saw Vorongil, Meta at his side. He smiled at her and received a wan smile in return. On the way up in the lift, Bart presented Raynor to Vorongil; the Lhari captain's eyebrows went up and his crest twitched when he heard that Raynor Three was off the *Multiphase*, but he said little. Bart was thinking of his plan, of Vorongil's kindness. Would Vorongil feel that Bart had deceived him, betrayed him, when he heard what Bart would say today?

Inside the inquiry room, four Lhari, imposing white-crested tall elfin figures in their metallic cloaks in clashing colours, sat across from four dignified men, stout and well-dressed, whom Bart believed to be the representatives of the Second Galaxy (Human) Federation of Intergalactic Trade. But the space beyond them was wholly filled with men, crowded together and

178

carrying stereo cameras, intercom equipment, the creepie-peepie of the on-the-spot news reporter, the transistorised transmitter of the space-commentator. The man who seemed to be foremost among the Trade Bureau dignitaries said, almost with apology:

'Mr. Steele, we had hoped to have this hearing quietly, without undue publicity. But the press seems to have got word, and we can't deny them the right to cover it, unless you object. You, and you alone, have the right to protest publicity on this matter. If you insist on your rights to privacy –'

'No, indeed,' said Bart clearly, 'I want as many people as possible to hear what I'm going to say.'

Raynor One came up to the bench. He said to Bart, and to the men of the commission, 'Bart, as your guardian I advise against it. There are going to be those who will call this just another publicity stunt. It's not going to do any good, either, to have it public knowledge that men have been trying to spy on the Lhari –'

'I want press coverage,' Bart repeated stubbornly, 'and as many star systems on the hookups and relays as possible.'

'He has the right to insist on that,' said one of the bureau members reluctantly, and the hearings began.

Bart told his story simply; his meeting with the elder Briscoe, his meeting with Raynor One – carefully not implicating Raynor One in the plot – Raynor Three's work in altering his appearance to that of a Lhari, and, skipping the details, the major events of his cruise aboard the *Swiftwing*. When he came to the account of the shift into warpdrive, he saw the faces of the pressmen watching, and realised that for them this was the story of the year – maybe of the century. *Humans can endure warpdrive!* But he went on, not soft-pedalling Montano's efforts to murder the Lhari crew, his own detection, the

179

trip to the Lhari worlds –

One of the men on the board interrupted, saying rather testily, 'What is the point of this lengthy narrative? You can give the whole story to the news media without our official sanction, if you wish to make it a heroic epic, young Steele. We have heard sufficient to prove your guilt, and that of Raynor, in the violation of an agreement –'

'Nevertheless, I want this to be official,' Bart said. 'I don't want to be mobbed when they discover that I have the stardrive.'

The effect was electric. The four Lhari across the board sat up; their white crests twitched. Vorongil stared, his grey eyes darkening with fear. Bart looked at him, and smiled kindly. One of the Lhari on the council leaned forward, shooting the question at him harshly.

'You did not discover the coordinates of Lharis! You did not discover the coordinates of the fuelling stop!'

'I did not,' Bart said quietly. 'I don't know them, and I have no intention of trying to find them out. We don't need to go to the Lhari galaxy to find the mineral that generates the warp frequencies that they call 'Catalyst A' and the Mentorians call *The Eighth Colour*. There is a green star called Meristem, and a spectroscopic analysis of that star, I'm sure, will find out what unknown elements it contains, and perhaps locate other stars with that element. There must be others in our galaxy, but the coordinates of the star Meristem are known to me.'

Vorongil was staring at him, his mouth open. He leaped up and cried out, shaking, 'But – they assured us that among your memories – there was nothing of danger to us –'

Compassionately, gently, Bart said, 'There wasn't – not that they knew about. I might never have remembered seeing a mineral that was a colour not found in the spectrum. Certainly, a memory like that

180

meant nothing to the Lhari Medics who emptied out my mind and turned over all my thoughts. You Lhari can't see any colour at all. So no one but I saw the colour of the mineral in the cave; you Lhari yourselves don't know that your fuel looks unlike anything else in the universe. So your Medics never questioned my memories of an eighth colour. To you, it's just another shade of grey, but under a light strong enough to blind any Mentorian eyes, it takes on a special colour –'

The conference broke up in disorder, the four Lhari clustering together in a furious babble, then hastily leaving the room. Bart stood waiting, feeling empty and cold. Vorongil's stare baffled him with unreadable emotion.

'You fool, you unspeakable young idiot!' Raynor One groaned. 'Why did you blurt it out like that before every newsmedia in the galaxy? Why, we could have had a monopoly on the stardrive – Eight Colours and Vega Interplanet!' As he saw the men of the press approaching with their microphones, lights, cameras and TV equipment, he gripped Bart urgently by the arm.

'We can still salvage something! Don't talk any more! Refer them to me – say I'm your guardian and your business manager – you can still make something of this –'

'That's just what I don't want to do,' Bart replied, and broke away from him to approach the newsmen.

'Yes, certainly, I'll answer all your questions, gentlemen.'

Raynor One flung up his hands in despair. But over the newsmen's shoulders Bart saw the glowing face of Meta, and smiled. She, at least, would understand. So would Raynor Three.

A page-boy touched Bart on the arm. 'Mr. Steele,' he said, 'You are to appear immediately before the World Council!'

'He's hardly of age – I'm his guardian – I have a right to speak for his interests –' Raynor One babbled, but Bart shook his head gently, and left him behind.

He was to be asked that question again and again in the days that followed, but his real answer was to Meta and Raynor Three, looking quietly past Raynor One and speaking to the news cameras that would carry his words all over the galaxy to men and Lhari.

'Why didn't I keep it for myself? Because there are always men like Montano, who in their mistaken pride will try to murder and steal for such things, and because there has been too much secrecy already. I want this knowledge to be used for the benefit of all men, not just a few. I want all men to have the stars.'

He had to tell his story again and again to the World Council and the hastily-summoned representatives of the entire Galactic Conference. At one point, a delegate from Vega actually rose and shouted at him that he had betrayed his home world and the whole human race.

'Don't you know the Lhari may fight a war over this?'

'No,' said Bart quietly, knowing his words would be quoted. 'Over something like this, I trust the Lhari more than I trust my own people. There won't be any war.'

But inwardly he sweated. He was very lonely; they kept him in what they called 'protective custody' during the whole nine days wonder of it, and he was as anxious as any when, one night, they let Raynor Three and Raynor One – as his guardians – come to visit him. There was, of course, now no chance of sending him to a prison planet for violation of trade agreement; public opinion would have crucified any man who suggested imprisoning the boy who had discovered a human-owned world containing deposits of Catalyst A. Bart could claim an 'explorer's share' of these deposits, which would be sizeable, he knew. But with all this, he hung fire, waiting with Raynor One for the hastily-

Lhari Council to arrive and state their official policy. And, at last, the announcement came.

'We are the first race to travel between the stars,' the bald, ancient Lhari face looked out from the vision-screen at Bart, and he remembered when he had stood before that face on Lharis, sick with defeat, feeling like a little boy sent home with a stolen cookie. 'We have had a long and triumphant time as masters of the stars. But triumph and power will sicken and stagnate the race which holds them alone too long. We reached this point once before, and a brave Lhari captain named Rhazon of Nedrum abandoned the safe ways of caution, and leaped into the dark gulf between the galaxies. Out of that blind leap in the blind dark came many good things. Trade with the human races. Our Mentorian friends and allies. A system of mathematics new to us, taking much of the hazard from our travel. Now again the Lhari have grown cautious and afraid, and it took a brave young man named Bartol to take a blind leap in the blind dark, and find his people a firm footing among the stars. It is too late for the Lhari to regret that we did not sooner extend you the hand of welcome, the invitation to join us in the endless realms of space. You have climbed up, uninvited, to join us. But there is room enough for us all; competition is the breath of trade, and life still holds many surprises for all of the living. I say to you: welcome to the stars.'

Even while Bart waited, speechless with the knowledge of success, the buzzer on his rooms rang and Raynor Three went quietly to open it. Bart looked up, then sprang to his feet in joy.

'Tom! Ringg! Meta!'

'Sure,' Tom exclaimed, 'We've got to celebrate,' but Bart stopped, looking past them.

'Captain Vorongil!' he said in wonder and awe, and went to greet the old Lhari. 'I thought – I was afraid you'd hate me, *rieko mori*.' The term of respect fell naturally from his lips.

'I did, for a time,' said the Lhari captain quietly. 'But I remembered the day we stood on Lharillis by the monument. And when the Lord of the High Council asked for my estimate of your people, I gave it.'

'I thought it sounded like you!' Bart burst out, and felt that his happiness was complete.

'And now,' Ringg cried, 'let's celebrate! Meta, you haven't even told him yet that he's free!'

But while the party got rolling, Bart wondered – free for what? What could come after? And after a little while he wandered out on the balcony and stood looking down over the spaceport city of Procyon Alpha to where the *Swiftwing* stood, huge, ovoid, beloved – renounced!

'What now, Bartol?' asked Vorongil's quiet voice at his elbow. 'You're famous – notorious. You're rich, and you're going to be a celebrity.'

He nodded. 'I was wishing I could just get away until all the excitement dies down.'

'Well,' said Vorongil, 'why don't you?'

'How, sir?'

'The *Swiftwing* ships out tonight, Bartol – Antares and beyond. It will be a couple of years before your Eight Colours can be made over into an interstellar line. According to Raynor One, he is your legal guardian and will have to handle all those details anyhow. You won't be of age for three years. But I've been thinking. Now that we Lhari must share space with your people, you'll need experienced men to run the ships. Unless we want the disasters born of trial and error, we Lhari had better help to train your people, quickly and well. Bartol, I want you to go back to Lharis on the *Swiftwing* with me. Not as an apprentice, but the representative of your own line, your own Eight Colours, to learn the ropes. To act as liaison between men and Lhari – at least until your own business demands your attention.'

'Captain – are you serious?' Bart could hardly believe it.

'Completely,' Vorongil said. Behind them on the balcony Tom appeared, making signals to Bart.

'Say yes! Say yes! *I* did!'

Bart's eyes suddenly filled. Out of defeat he had won a success beyond his greatest hopes. But he did not feel proud; he only felt a heavy responsibility. Whether good or bad came of the gift he had snatched from the stars would rest in large measure on his own shoulders. He was going back to space – to learn the responsibility that went with it.

'I accept,' he said gravely.

'Oh boy!' Tom yelled, and dragged Ringg into a sort of war-dance of exuberant celebration. After a moment Bart felt Meta's hand in his. They looked over the balcony at the Lhari spaceport and he put his arms around her shoulders. Tom pointed at the flaring glow of the spaceport gates.

'Here, by grace of the Lhari, stands the doorway to all the stars,' he quoted. 'Well, maybe they were here first. But look out! We're coming!'

A doorway to the stars. Bart had crossed that doorway once, frightened and alone. He spoke, half aloud:

'*Dad, if you could only know!*' The first interstellar ship of the Eight Colours line was to bear the name of the *Rupert Steele*, but that was years in the future. Now, looking at the *Swiftwing*, looking round at Meta, at Ringg, at Tom, at Raynor Three and Vorongil, who would all be his shipmates and companions in the new world they were building, he felt suddenly lonely again.

'Come in, Bart. It's your party,' Meta said softly. He looked down at the Mentorian girl's hand lying in his; suddenly he knew he would never be alone again.

His arm around Meta, his friends – man and Lhari –

at his shoulders, he went back to the celebration to plan the first intergalactic expedition to the stars.

ISAAC ASIMOV

SPACE RANGERS

Four exciting sci-fi novels featuring David Starr, Space Ranger:

SPACE RANGER

When an alien force begins to poison the inhabitants of Earth, David Starr, Space Ranger, feels compelled to overcome it. Even if he must face death himself...

PIRATES OF THE ASTEROIDS

Twenty-five years ago, a vicious band of space privateers murdered David Starr's parents. Now, nothing can stop him as he begins his perilous journey towards his long awaited vengeance.

LIGHTNING

ISAAC ASIMOV

SPACE RANGERS

OCEANS OF VENUS

On Venus, an underwater colony of earthmen is threatened with disaster. Can David Starr, Space Ranger, survive long enough to face the evil menace of the Oceans of Venus...?

THE BIG SUN OF MERCURY

On the barren planet of Mercury the mighty power of the sun is harnessed by a network of wire, creating a giant powerhouse to send solar energy crackling across space. Some unseen enemy is sabotaging the Mercury project. Now it must be David Starr's mission to find that enemy...

LIGHTNING

WOLF OF SHADOWS

WHITLEY STRIEBER

At the beginning of a nuclear winter, a desperate mother and her daughter join the formidable Wolf of Shadows as he leads his pack south. Their journey is a dark odyssey through the frozen wasteland that was once the United States. Only the pack bonding sustains them in their search for a place where life can be reborn.

"Skilfully told."
 Junior Bookshelf

LIGHTNING

COLD FEET

JEAN RICHARDSON

I turned to look back, and saw that the big old farmhouse building was gone, and that all that was left was the low shape of a cottage or hut, no bigger than one of our barns. But there wasn't time to think about that. Water was lapping round my bare feet. I heard a massive creaking and could just make out the shape of the enormous bulk moving, the hull, masts and all, and riggings, and straining sails, of a galleon.

There was the cry again. This time I knew even before the light came up again what it was. A child was in the water, and he was shouting for help.

Haunting tales to thrill and chill from Robert Westall, Joan Aiken, Antonia Barber, Philip Pullman, Pamela Oldfield, Alison Prince, Jean Richardson and Berlie Doherty.

"Most distinguished."
  The Times Educational Supplement

LIGHTNING

THE OTHER SIDE OF DARK

JOAN LOWERY NIXON

When Stacy McAdams wakes in a hospital room to discover she has been in a coma for the past four years, her problems are only just beginning.

An innocent thirteen-year-old trapped in the body of a mature seventeen-year-old, Stacy has a lot of catching up to do. She yearns for the familiarity of her previous world.

Stacy is heartbroken to discover that her mother has been killed. Murdered by the same stranger who shot Stacy four years ago – and she is the only eye-witness. The only eye-witness to a murderer who hasn't been caught...

LIGHTNING

SAFE, STRONG AND STREETWISE

HELEN BENEDICT

SAFE, STRONG AND STREETWISE takes a bold look at some of the problems faced by teenagers today. What is sexual abuse? How can you defend yourself against it? Who can you turn to for help and advice? How should you react if you are physically attacked? All these important questions and more are answered in a realistic and constructive way, using accounts given by young people about difficult situations they have had to face.

"It's the ultimate street-safety guide."
  Lenny Henry

LIGHTNING